I0620598

Theirs To Treasure

Beyond Monogamy:Book One

Marissa Dobson

Copyright ©2014 Marissa Dobson
All rights reserved. No part of this publication may be reproduced, stored in a retrieval
system, or transmitted in any form or by any means, electronic, mechanical, photocopying,
recording, or otherwise, without the prior written permission of the publisher.
Published by Dobson Ink
Printed in the United States of America
ISBN-13: 978-1-939978-56-1

Dedication

To everyone who lives their lives on their own terms. Don't worry about what the world thinks of you, instead embrace what makes you happy. Cherish your loved ones and live each day as if it might be your last.

I'd like to thank my wonderful husband, Thomas, for his support and for encouraging me to write Theirs to Treasure. Thank you Rosa Sophia, Brynna Curry, and Kimberly Wise for your work on this book. Without each of you it wouldn't be as wonderful as it is.

To my readers for all your support. I hope you enjoy this glimpse into the future in the Beyond Monogamy series. Finally I'd like to thank you to my wonderful street team, for all your hard work, dedication, and support. I love you guys.

Chapter One

During the winter of 2115, storm after storm dumped piles of snow until Paris Nelson thought she'd never see the green grass again. She vowed she was taking a vacation at the first sign of nice weather, somewhere far from her office. To work from home seemed like a dream but it also had her working longer than normal hours. Day or night if she wasn't working she was thinking about work, and the fact that her office was adjoined to her bedroom made it hard to separate life from work.

She leaned back in her leather office chair and looked out at the beautiful mountains with their snow covered caps. Even through the latest snowstorm, the mountains called to her. When was the last time she'd gone skiing, or snowboarding? Too long. Since the world had changed, the family's dating company—Beyond Monogamy—had taken off. People had lived the lifestyle in private, but now they were going public and seeking help to find the perfect match. Good for business, bad for her life outside the office.

It was amazing to think her fathers were on the battleground to make all of this possible. They'd fought for the rights to live a polyandry lifestyle, the right for one wife to have multiple husbands, as well as polygamy—one husband with multiple wives. Her father, Mathew, was one of the lawyers fighting the legal grounds while Paul had taken other routes to make the future possible. Making their relationship public while it was still illegal had given her parents a rough start, but they made it possible for Paris and her bother London to live this life if they chose to. Not to mention the countless other couples and future generations they paved the way for.

"Paris, we need to talk." Paul, one of her fathers, stood in the door frame looking stressed.

"What's wrong? Is it Mom? Something happen at her doctor's appointment?" She sat up straighter in her chair, giving Dad her full attention.

"The doctor ordered another round of the chemotherapy and radiation to begin immediately." Her father stepped into her office until he stood just in front of the large cherry wood desk. "You've been cooped up in this office working too much."

"What are you getting at?" Her forehead creased with suspicion as she watched her father lead into something. It had to be something big for him to go through all that trouble.

"We've been thinking it's time for you to get out more. I have a client I was supposed to meet with in Thermopolis, Wyoming, but with your mom's treatments and Mathew working on that murder trial, I need someone to take my place. These are very important clients, and they've asked that someone come to them."

"Why not send London? He's the one who normally deals with the face to face stuff; I'm the matchmaker behind the scenes."

"This client is special." He tipped his head and looked at the stack of paperwork she was working on. "It's better than what you're working on here, and these can wait until you're back, or you can give them to London to complete. Plus, you deserve to get out of this office once in a while. Point is, I really need you to take this trip for me. I don't want to leave your mom right now. The chemo has been bad enough but with radiation, it's going to be worse. Mathew and I both need to be with her."

"Who's the client?" She relented without much of a fight because she understood her parents needed to be together. Cancer was a bitch, and her dads wanted to be there for anything Mom needed. She leaned forward to the computer to pull up the file she'd need once he told her the client's name.

"You won't find him in the system. I've been keeping this one close to the vest because of who the client is. I didn't need London finding out because he'd want to deal with it and that's just not happening. Oh, that boy." He shoved his hands into his pockets and shook his head.

"London isn't that bad, he just likes to party a little too much. There's never been any problem with him and the business. He shows the clients a good time when they need it. It's more than the rest of us do." Even if her baby brother got on her last nerve sometimes, she still felt the need to defend him. "Maybe we should all take a page from his book, we work too hard. I know you and Dad laid back a little since Mom's been sick, but maybe once the treatments are complete you should think about taking her away for a few days. She could use it."

"None of this has been fair on you." He leaned against the edge of her desk. "My little girl, running the company while we care for Mom. You rarely ever leave the house unless it's for work. What kind of life is that for you?"

"I love my work and wouldn't change that. You know if there's anything you need, just let me know and you can consider it done. You need to focus on Mom, she's top priority. I can handle Beyond Monogamy…and even London if I need to." She grabbed her notebook and pen. "Now who's this secret client?"

"Aiden Dalton."

She gasped, certain she'd heard him wrong. "Not Aiden Dalton, the former pro-football player?"

"The one and only. He received my number from a colleague and contacted me directly. Now you understand why I can't have your brother take this *and* why it needs to be kept quiet. I've got the basic information he provided on this." He dangled a jump drive from between his fingers until she took it. "None of this can go into the system. For now, it's just between us, Mathew, and Mom. Don't say a word to London."

"Oh, believe me, now I understand why you didn't want him to take this client. He's always been a huge fan of Aiden's, even after he blew out his knee and had to give up playing." She looked at the drive and wondered what she'd find on it, while her mind had already jumped to conclusions of its own. "How many wives is he looking for?"

"My sweet daughter, you've got it wrong. He's only looking for one…and before you ask why he'd used our company if not for multiple partners, it's because he's partnered with two other men and *they're* looking for one wife."

"One wife?" The question came out lighter than she had expected it. "Sorry, Dad, it's just not what I've expected. The media always portrayed him as a bad boy and something of a ladies' man. To think he's willing to settle down with one woman and share her with two other men is hard to believe."

"Remember what the media tried to do to the company? It could have been done to him, too." He shrugged. "I don't know much yet. I've only spoken to Kain, Aiden's lawyer, who is *also* one of the partners. You need to go, gather the rest of the information, and if you feel that Beyond Monogamy cannot help them, I'll trust your judgment. However if we can, it could be the hit we need to take the company to the next level."

"We've already got more business than we can handle."

"We'll have to hire more staff." When she shook her head, he added, "Employees are not overrated. Even *you* can't run this company on your own. If you tried, you'd burn out. Have you given more thoughts to hiring an assistant?"

"Dad, that just not me. I'm too controlling, I would be double checking everything she did."

"You need someone to help you. You're working too much." He cupped his hand over hers. "Since Mom's been sick, you've picked up the duties Mathew and I used to handle. It's not fair on you. I had hoped London would have helped you with some of them, but he's too busy acting as *entertainment director*."

"It's what family does," she insisted, ignoring his last comment. "Plus, I love what I do and that makes the long hours worth it. Just know I'm going to take a few days off once the weather is nice again. I want to sink my toes into the sand. London will have to manage by himself for a few days. Now, back to business. When am I supposed to meet with Aiden, Kain, and the other man?"

"The plane will be ready for you at ten tomorrow morning. You'll arrive at a private airport just on the outskirts of Thermopolis, and Kain will be there to meet you. You should be able to wrap up what you need to do by dinner time, and the pilot will be on standby to make the return trip when you're ready."

"Very well. Then I better get this stack of paperwork complete." She scooted her chair closer to the desk, prepared to return to the tasks at hand.

"Okay, I can take a hint. Let me know if there's anything I can do. Being here with Mom doesn't mean I can't do some of this paperwork." He rose from the edge of the desk where he had been leaning.

"It's fine, Dad. You need to focus on Mom. Plus, this is just the standard check, and one client I need to go through some matches for. What I don't finish tonight I can get done on the plane tomorrow." Her cell phone rang, giving her the excuse she needed to get back to work. She glanced at the screen and saw one of her clients' names. The call could wait, but knowing Dad, he'd hang around if she didn't take it. "If you'll excuse me, Dad, I need to take this."

"I'll see you for dinner tonight."

She nodded as her father left her office. When he reached the door, she brought the phone to her ear. "Hello, Carter. I was just about to call you."

"Lily and I were wondering if you found us a potential match. We're planning a trip to visit her family. If you've found someone who isn't local, we'd like to see about meeting with her while we're traveling."

"Actually, I did." She clicked a few buttons on the keyboard and brought his file up on the screen. "The woman I have selected for you is named Dana. Looking over both of your files, I believe she'd be the perfect fit for you. She lives in Florida, and though she hasn't been in a relationship like this herself, she was raised with two mothers."

"Would she be willing to relocate? With the business, I couldn't, so that's a big thing for us, and Florida is across the country."

"She's willing, and understands you have a chain of hardware stores in Arizona. That won't be an issue. She's anxious to meet you and Lily and has even offered to fly out there." She opened Diane's file, creating a side by side display on the computer screen. "I can email her picture and information for you to look over. If you'd like to arrange a meeting, or speak with her over the phone, I can provide the contact information."

"Shoot the file over and we'll look at it this evening. If she's the one, we'll be in Georgia visiting Lily's family and we can meet with her." The hesitation in Carter's voice reminded her of why she had taken him on as a personal client. She hadn't let anyone else, not even her fathers, deal with his request.

Normally her clients were excited when she told them there was a match, but Carter had been down this road before and it showed in his reservation. Before coming to Beyond Monogamy, he had tried another less credible company that hadn't screened their clients properly. Carter and Lily had been through Hell and back with the prospective mate before they were able to distance themselves. It had taken them nearly two years before they were willing to try again, and Paris was making this her personal priority. She had double checked Diane, digging even deeper than normal to ensure there was nothing alarming in her past. With every check, Diane had come up clean—not even a speeding ticket. Paris had been doing this long enough that she had a six sense about matching; she could even feel it in her bones, and she knew Diane was the right match for Carter and Lily.

She had ended the call and emailed him the file before she picked up the jump drive Dad had given her. She was anxious to read what was on the file but there were still other things she needed to deal with before she could focus on that. She forced herself to lay it aside and focus on the paperwork she had been working on when Dad had entered. She needed to finish searching through matches for another client so she could settle on one, and that needed to be done before her flight in the morning.

The paperwork detailing the couple who was searching for another wife sat on top with the possible matches to the side. Trying to match Greta and Bob with another woman had been more challenging than most. How Greta and Bob made their relationship work in the first place was beyond Paris. They were almost completely different people, and everything she'd learned in the matchmaking business told her they couldn't possibly work, yet somehow they had for over five years. Now they wanted to add to their family, something they'd wanted to do for years, but with Bob's career as a police officer, it hadn't been possible until now.

"Hey, sis." London leaned against the door frame. "I passed Dad when I came in and he said you might need a hand with some paperwork. What can I do for you?"

"You know, little brother, you might be just the person I'm looking for. Are you familiar with Greta and Bob's file?"

"Yeah, aren't they in Maine and looking for a wife?" He strolled toward her desk, his hands in the front pockets of his jeans.

She nodded. "You think outside of the box, maybe you can figure out which of these three would be the best fit. Each time I look at the women, I talk myself out of the one I thought I settled on. Each of them would be perfect for either Greta or Bob, but I'm not sure completely perfect for both."

11

"I could do some research and settle on one so you can get to the rest of this stuff." He nodded to the papers scattered around the desk. "Anything else you need?"

"What's with the change? You have a workload of your own and don't normally offer to help."

"Dad told me about Mom's upcoming treatment. I want both our dads to feel confident that we can handle the company so they can focus on Mom."

She placed her hand over his. "Little brother, I think you're finally growing up. Thank you. If you can handle them I'll be able to deal with everything else."

"Consider it done." He stood back up with the papers in hand. "Dad wanted me to remind you that we're expected at dinner."

"I told him I'd be there." She shook her head. "I've got to go out of town in the morning, it's just a day trip, but if anything changes with Mom I want you to call me. I know our dads won't unless it's something serious, since I'm meeting with a client, but I want to know. Okay?"

"You know I will." He nodded. "I didn't see anything in the book about you traveling this week."

"It was unexpected." Not wanting to rouse his suspicions, she added, "I just need to smooth some ruffled feathers and assure him we can take care of all his needs."

"Well, if you need to show him a good time I can give you a list of the area's hotspots."

"I appreciate that, but that's not my scene and I don't think the client wants that either. Though I'll keep it in mind if that comes up." She didn't want him to wonder about the client, or start to ask questions, so she quickly changed the subject. "Now, if there's anything I can do for you, just let me know."

"I've got it under control, Dottie makes sure of that."

She nodded, knowing his personal assistant Dottie wouldn't allow the clients to suffer while London was enjoying the nightlife and showing the clients a good time. She made sure he did the real work as well, and for that, the whole family was thankful. Maybe Mom's latest cancer treatment was forcing him to grow up, because he'd never offered to take any of Paris's work no matter how busy she was.

She leaned back in her office chair letting her gaze drift back to the window. Since cancer had touched their lives, things had grown a little darker around the house. While London let himself get sucked into the party scene to forget what was going on with their mother, she had drowned herself in work. That needed to change, for both of them. She had to have a life outside of work, so maybe Dad was right. Maybe it was time to hire an assistant.

Chapter Two

Paris skimmed the file for the hundredth time, mentally quizzing herself to make sure she had the details right for each of the clients. She wanted to have the basics down, allowing her to cut to the important questions she needed to ask. The biggest one weighing on her thoughts was *why*. Why had they chosen to find a woman together? Especially Aiden, who had women fighting over him, clamoring to dance with him at nightclubs. Why was he seeking Beyond Monogamy's help to find him a wife?

She tried to empty her thoughts of any preconceived impressions the media caused. After all, her family was no stranger to yellow journalism. Reporters, journalists—they all wrote what they knew would sell. It didn't have to be the truth, as she had already learned by reading the tabloids.

When the company emerged from the shadows and started helping people find matches, the tabloids had reported all kinds of ugly stuff about the whole family. Maybe that was what happened with Aiden. Either way, it was her job to find out. If he still had the playboy attitude, she wasn't willing to help him. The company had a reputation to uphold. It would not be brought down because of an unsuccessful pairing.

"Miss Nelson, we'll be landing in ten minutes." Jake Thornstead, the pilot, announced over the intercom.

She gathered the printouts for each of the men into the manila folder to place it in her laptop bag and prepare for landing. The picture of the three men standing in front of a sprawling log home caught her attention. She had assumed it was the home of the three men, where they had settled down after Aiden retired, but it wasn't the home that caught her attention. It was the smiles on each of their faces. Each had their own appeals, while all of them were easy on the eyes. She'd at least have something nice to look at while she was there.

She scolded herself for even thinking it. She was there to do a job; it shouldn't matter if the men were good looking or not. Though according to the heat rushing up her cheeks, it mattered a whole lot. Looking at the picture of the three of them made her feel as if they were looking into her soul. Their eyes penetrated beyond her business façade, seeming to peer into what she had kept hidden all these years.

"That's crazy," she whispered before shoving the picture into the folder with the rest of the documents just as the plane adjusted its altitude for landing. "Pull it together. You can't be flushed when you meet them."

She grabbed her compact mirror from the bag to check her makeup and hair one final time, telling herself she was doing it because she needed to make a good impression for the company's sake. She ran her fingers through her long brown hair, fluffing it into position before tossing the mirror back in her bag and leaning into her chair.

The few moments she had while they made their landing might be the only reprieve she received from work, because after she was done here there wasn't a doubt in her mind the work had already begun piling up on her desk back home. They never had time off without paying for it later, especially now that it was only she and London doing most of the matchmaking. Where five had done the job before, now only two remained. Best case scenario, her mother would go into remission and the three parents could once again resume their work within the company, easing the load off her and London. On the other hand, if the treatments continued they might have to look into hiring help—especially an assistant for her.

The plane touched down on the runway as she continued to ponder the idea of actually hiring an assistant. She wasn't sure she could give up enough control in order to let the assistant work. If she just double checked everything once the assistant completed the work it would take twice as much time. What she needed was someone like Dottie, someone she could trust to do the job correctly.

When the plane came to a halt, she took a deep breath and stood. Jake would finish shutting down the engine before he opened the plane door for her, but she needed to stand to work off some of the tension in her shoulders. She wasn't sure why she was so worked up about meeting these clients, and the best she could come up with was because it swayed from the normal routine of things. They didn't usually travel to clients, especially not without more information on them. This meeting was like an interview. While she evaluated them, they would be doing the same with her and the company as a whole. She needed to make a good impression on them because her father was right; this could open all kinds of doors for the company.

"Miss Nelson." Jake called to her as he emerged from the cockpit, placing his captain's hat over his dark brown hair which showed early sprinklings of gray throughout. "Are you ready?"

"Yes, thank you." She slipped her arms into her coat and grabbed her bag off the seat before she proceeded up the wide aisle of the private jet. "I'm not sure how long I'll be."

"Don't worry about that. The plane will be gassed and ready to go when you are."

"Thank you." She gave him a quick smile because she knew that no matter what happened at this meeting Jake would be waiting, ready to rush her back to the safety of the Nelson house. Not that waiting was that big of a hardship for him, since the Nelsons had made sure the new jet had sleeping quarters for themselves, as well as a private area for Jake where he could rest while waiting for them to return from whatever business they had to attend to.

He unlocked the door and let the steps unfold. "Good luck with your business dealings, Miss Nelson."

"Thank you." She buttoned one of the middle buttons on her coat to keep the wind from blowing it open as she came down the plane's steps and made her way to the black SUV waiting for her.

Her heels clicked off the last step as a man came around the SUV, his black cowboy hat slung low on his head, hiding his eyes. He was clad in a chocolate brown jacket, with the blanket lining showing around the collar that fell at his hips. His long legs were encased in stonewashed jeans; a pair of black cowboy boots perfected his image.

"You must be Mr. Fitzgerald." She held out her hand to him.

"Kain, please. You must be Mr. Nelson's assistant." He glanced past her toward the jet.

"Actually, I'm his daughter, Paris. I thought my father had called you to explain that I would be taking his place."

"No, he didn't." Kain crossed his arms over his chest, suddenly making himself more intimidating. "Considering I've done all my dealings with him to date, I expected him to show up for this meeting." His tone let her know he was somewhat put off by the fact that Paul had not come personally.

"I understand, and on behalf of my family I'd like to apologize for someone not calling you before I arrived. There's an urgent situation that required his attention." She hated that she felt the need to apologize but she wasn't going into personal details on why her father had stayed home. "If you'd prefer to wait until he can make the trip personally, I can return to the jet and be on my way." She raised an eyebrow at him, almost daring him to tell her to get out of there, because she'd be damn sure that her father heard about it, and

Beyond Monogamy wouldn't be taking them on as clients as a result. They weren't into playing games for the spoiled rich, not when there were real clients who wanted and needed their help; those were the ones who truly mattered to her.

"No." He shook his head. "Aiden has been looking forward to getting this process started. I just hope you're not wasting our time. I'd rather not complete this interview again with Mr. Nelson."

"I assure you that will not happen. I'm going to handle your matchmaking experience. Now if you wouldn't mind, I'd like to get into the SUV and be on our way. It's cold out here."

The corner of his mouth turned up into the first smile she had seen from him. "Growing up in Thermopolis, I'm used to the cold and tend to forget about it." He pulled open the passenger door and waited for her to get in. When she did, he shut the door and went around the SUV to the driver's side.

She watched him as he climbed into the large SUV and tried to hide her surprise. He wasn't what she expected from his file. Kain looked like he should have been working security for Aiden, or possibly in some aspect of law enforcement, not a lawyer. He was intimidating, and when he stared down at her, it was as if he was looking through her. If she had some deep dark secret, she'd have confessed under the scrutiny of his gaze. Though that might come in handy for him during a legal trail. He was just so different from her own lawyer father, Mathew.

"Aiden and Cody are waiting for you at the house. I had some business to attend to in town before meeting the plane, so I was elected to pick you up," he explained, throwing the vehicle into drive.

"I appreciate you picking me up." She forced herself to look away from him and focused her attention outside the window. "It's beautiful here."

"I wouldn't want to live anywhere else." He turned off the small landing strip and onto a gravel road. "This is actually my brother's land, he purchased it from our parents when they wanted to downsize now that all of us are older. It's when we put in the landing strip. We're basically the only ones who use it, but when Aiden's career was more active it was almost mandatory for us so we could get home. Many times we would only have a few days to get away, and flying into Denver, then the small plane to Casper…it was just too much, especially in the winter when you could end up snowbound."

"Sometimes those little trips, a few days of rest and relaxation, make all the difference." She ran her hand over the leather laptop bag she had on her lap. What did she know about vacations? She never took time off. The day before, she'd thought about getting away once the weather was nice, but it had been more than a year since she'd actually taken a day off. Her mother's cancer had changed things for all of them, and the one thing she had given up was personal and vacation time. If she wasn't working, she was helping her fathers care for her mother.

"They can be, except when it's filled with more things to do. Now that Aiden has retired, there's a different pace to life. One I didn't know I missed until I had it again." He glanced over at her. "We have a twenty minute drive to the house, but if you'd like to stop in town for anything, we can."

"I'm fine, thank you. I'd just like to meet the others. I'll meet with all of you together and then I'll speak with each of you separately as well."

"Well, we have some time if there's anything you'd like to ask me now." He sped by a house just as a man was grabbing stuff from the mailbox, and he waved his hand full of envelopes. "My brother," he explained, returning the wave.

"It's not how we normally do things, but we might as well put this time together to good use." She unclasped the buckle on her bag and grabbed her notebook.

"Why do you prefer to meet with the clients together first?"

"That way we only have to explain how the process works, what to expect, and it allows both sides to get an idea of each other. Then we don't have to waste any time. Once some clients find out how the process works, what information will be needed, and how far we dig into everyone's backgrounds, they decide to explore other options. That being said, we look into each client's background as protection for everyone involved in the matchmaking experience. We don't want to match you with someone with mental issues or someone who is only after your money. We want the match to work, just as you do."

"It's one of the reasons we chose your company." He turned onto a paved road before looking over at her. "Beyond Monogamy has a reputation of being thorough, and I've read the matches tend to last."

"Dad mentioned you were referred to us by a colleague, so it's always nice when a client does research before contacting us. It shows they're serious about finding someone." She flipped the notebook open to a blank page. "Do you have any questions I might be able to answer?"

"How about one about you?" He didn't give her time to tell him this wasn't about her before he continued. "I know it's a family business, but why do you do it? You seem like a sweet lady who could do anything she wanted. Why work in a business that is so controversial?"

"Joy." She smiled, thinking about the happiness she could see in the faces of her clients when a match worked out. "It might be a family business, but my parents would have been supportive if I had chosen to go into another field. I had never even considered it. I love my work. There's nothing better than bringing happiness and joy to others. To see the love in their eyes and knowing I brought them together. Many of the clients I have matched remain in touch with me, which is nice because I get to see how things work out for them. I have a board in my office just for pictures of happy clients, and over the years, many of them have sent pictures of their children. It's the reason I knew the battle was worth it."

"What battle?"

"The legal battle. Mathew fought it in the courts, but the rest of us were behind him all the way. We worked to make this lifestyle legal for those who wanted to live it because love isn't just limited to one person. Sometimes you need multiple people in a relationship to make it work, each giving each other something different, to make a complete and strong bond. Being on the front lines of this battle brought more attention to my family than I ever thought possible, but it helped others come forward and embrace what they truly wanted out of life. Don't get me wrong. There were times we were concerned for our safety, that my parents might be arrested, but in the end, it worked out. Well, it is working out."

"Is?" He glanced toward her.

"The threatening letters still come by the truck load, but we take precautions to keep us safe."

"Don't you ever fear that one day someone opposed to the choices your family and the company represents will intend to harm you?"

"If you mean are there times I'm afraid for my life, or the lives of those I love, the simple answer is yes. I was raised to stand up for what I believe in, and I've seen the good things this lifestyle as to offer. My dads made sure I could handle myself. I think they were rougher on me because I'm their only daughter. Self-defense lessons nearly every day growing up, even now we still work though the routine at least once a week. I think I was ten when they first took me to the range and taught me gun safety. When I turned twenty-one they made sure I received my concealed weapon permit. Even with all that, we have security at the house, and they usually travel with us when we're meeting clients."

"Then why did you come alone today?"

She turned slightly in her seat to look at him. "This situation called for a little more privacy, and after my father and I spoke about it he felt I would be fine. He assured me that one of you would pick me up at the landing strip and would take me back. With Jake—the pilot—standing by for when I wanted to leave, we thought it would be acceptable to make this journey without my normal security detail." She raised an eyebrow at him. "Though I'll say this now…if you or anyone else here have other ideas on why you brought me here, I suggest you rethink it. I'm not just some woman who needs someone to protect her. I do a fine job of that myself."

"How could we have called you here for other means when we didn't know you'd be the one who would arrive? We expected Paul Nelson."

"It wouldn't have been unheard of to invite someone under the pretense of seeking their services only to hold them hostage to use them as leverage to try to get the new law reversed. If it were anyone else other than Mr. Dalton, it could be said that you sought a ransom."

"If you thought any of that, you wouldn't have come."

She nodded. "You're right. If there was even the slightest doubt. I wouldn't have come, not even with a team of security guards at my back. I'd rather pass over a client, no matter who they are, and live another day than risk myself or my family. After all, as much as I love the work I do, this is just a job, and family is so much more than that."

She wasn't sure what to think of Kain. One minute he seemed to open up to her, to let down his hard exterior, and then it was as if she was back at square one. He was distant, and the way he phrased things put her on edge as if she was on trial. If he did this with a prospective match, it could make for an icy beginning, one that might never get past the first step.

Once she got a better understanding of the others and decided if she was actually going to take them on as a client, she'd have to sit down and talk to him about his off-putting attitude. Otherwise, they were wasting their time.

Chapter Three

The SUV pulled up in front of a sprawling log home with wide windows that took advantage of the amazing Wyoming views. It was set on a mountain, looking down on the town and across to the next mountain peaks. The picture of the three of them before it didn't do the house justice. Huge logs the size of Paris's waist made up the external walls in a warm honey color that stood out perfectly against the snowy backdrop. The outside was stunning, and she couldn't wait to step inside because she was sure there was more beauty within.

"We had this house custom built for our needs before Aiden retired, but it's nice to live here full time," Kain explained as he observed her awe.

"It's beautiful."

He looked back at the house as if he was seeing it through her eyes and smiled. "It is, but to fully appreciate it you have to see the inside."

"Is there a reason you're keeping our guest waiting in this weather?" A man with dark brown hair, and the deepest chocolate brown eyes she had ever seen, came toward them.

"Miss Nelson, this is Cody Knight." He shifted his intense stare to Cody. "She's Mr. Nelson's daughter and is here representing Beyond Monogamy."

"Welcome." Cody held out his hand to her. "Don't let Kain put you off. His bark is worse than his bite."

She returned his smile as she accepted his offered hand. "It's nice to meet you. Please call me Paris."

His smile showed off the boyish good looks that hadn't shown in the picture and she had to admit those perfect dimples in his cheeks made her knees weak. If a match for these three was going to work, she might need to get Cody at the forefront of it. His welcoming smile and easy attitude would make someone feel more comfortable than Kain's cold stare.

"Come on. Let's get you inside where it's warm. Aiden should be done with his phone call by now and we can get started." He led her across the cobblestone driveway to the stairs leading up to the deck and front door.

"I'd like to meet with all three of you first and then each of you separately."

Cody turned enough to look back at Kain. "You didn't tell her?"

"Tell me what?" she questioned before Kain could answer.

"Aiden has requested to meet with you first. He had planned to meet the plane but an unexpected business matter came up that had him otherwise engaged," Cody explained as they made their way up the stairs.

She nodded as he opened the front door and she stepped into the warmth of the house. The heels of her boots clicked against the foyer's marble floors as she moved deeper inside. The logs from outside continued within, but everything else was warm and inviting.

"Let me take your coat."

Without looking at Cody, she slipped it off and handed it to him. Her gaze scanned the space she could see. Through the large opening, she spotted a living area with a kitchen just off to the right, open and welcoming. Only a large kitchen bar with wood bar stools separated the two spaces.

"I've got something to do. Show her into his office." Kain slipped past them and headed down the hallway to the right.

Cody shook his head before looking back at her. "I swear, he does have a better personality hidden under that attitude."

"I think he's upset that I had to take my father's place today due to unfortunate circumstances, and I don't think it helped matters that he didn't call before I showed up, to let the three of you know."

"It wouldn't have changed anything. Kain is very protective, and he doesn't like change, but he'll come around." He handed her the laptop bag she had set aside while she took off her coat. "If you'll follow me, I'm sure Aiden is wondering what the delay is since he probably saw the SUV pull up from his office."

She slipped the bag over her shoulder and followed him. "I understand he's put out that I came instead of my father, but I'm still here to get the job done. If he'd prefer to go with another company because it didn't work out how he wanted, that's his choice."

"No," a deep voice announced from a room just steps before them.

"That would be Aiden." Cody nodded to the office. "I'll make myself scarce while the two of you discuss business, but I look forward to sitting down with you shortly."

She watched him disappear down the hallway before the voice from the room caught her attention again. There behind a large cherry wood desk was Aiden, looking just like all of the pictures she had seen of him in the media. His blond hair was spiked on top while the rest was buzzed close to the scalp. His light purple shirt, almost a pale lavender, had the collar button undone, making him appear more approachable.

"Please come in. I'm Aiden Dalton." He came around his desk and she caught a glimpse of the blue jeans that encased his long legs. "You're not Paul, but I'm assuming you're with Beyond Monogamy."

"Yes." She held out her hand to him. "Paris Nelson, his daughter. Due to unforeseen circumstances he was unable to make it today." She was getting tired of explaining her presence and where her father was. It reminded her why they preferred to meet with everyone together first instead of going over the same things repeatedly.

"I'm sure that pleased Kain, but I have no doubt you'll do a great job. Please have a seat."

"Normally we prefer to meet with all of the clients together, then conduct private interviews," she explained once again.

"I understand, but I'd like to speak with you before the others join us." He waited for her to take a seat before he leaned against the edge of his desk. "I'm assuming you've done your research, you know who I am, so you'll understand how delicate the situation is."

"I knew who you were before I opened your file. I might not be much of a football fan and I rarely have television on, but my brother London is a big supporter of yours. You might not play any longer, but he'd still flip over backwards to meet you. Which is why I'm here instead of him. Your request is being kept quiet, only my parents and I know about it or even that I'm here."

"I appreciate that." He smirked. "While I'm thankful to have fans, playing football was never about that. I did it because I loved the game, and when I had to give it up I thought my life was over." He rubbed his knee, as if just thinking about it made the pain return.

"Maybe it's because I've never been a diehard sports fan, but there's more to life than football."

He nodded. "You're right, which is why you're here. Since I got out of the game I realized how much life has to offer. There's so much I've been missing. Which brings me to my point. We're looking for someone we can spend the rest of our lives with, not someone who can only see the dollar signs or the fame from being with someone with my background."

"I understand that and will do everything in my power to find you the perfect match. You should know it's not going to happen overnight. Simply due to your career, your situation is more advanced than some of the other cases we've worked with, so I want to take extra care to make sure it's perfect. The first step is for me to talk to all of you, to gather a better understanding of what you want and need from someone." She scooted forward on the chair. "I'm assuming that since the three of you have decided to do this together that you've spoken about what you want as a group, what you're willing to sacrifice in order to make it work. No one woman is going to have everything all three of you are looking for, so we need to have the most important factors and go from there."

"We have. Each of us have our own personalities, wants, and needs, but when it comes to finding the perfect woman for us we're on the same page. Though before we get started on that, I'll call them here."

"That was it?" She managed to keep the surprise from her voice but she felt her eyes widen.

"Your father called after Kain left to let me know you'd be taking his place today. So I only wanted to make sure you understood about my career and the challenges it would cause in your search."

"If you knew, why didn't you tell Kain?" She nearly shot out of her chair. "For a moment I thought he was going to ask me to get on the plane and go back to where I came from. He was pretty put out that I took my father's place today."

"Cell phone service is spotty in the mountains and when I tried I couldn't reach him. I figured it would be a nice surprise to keep him on his toes so I just left him a message that I wanted to speak with you when you arrived."

"That's evil, do you know that?" She shook her head and laughed. "Poor guy."

"It's good to keep Kain on his toes. He's been with me for over a dozen years as my lawyer. While he was working his way through law school he did security for me occasionally."

"With a stare like his I have no doubt he was good at that. When he looks at you, it's as if he's looking through you. Let's put it this way, he's not a guy most would test."

"He was very good at his job, even after he became my lawyer, he was good to have by my side when I needed extra security. Even now that I'm retired he won't give up the role of bodyguard." He stood and walked around the desk. "We'll meet in here unless you prefer to gather around the dining room table."

"This is fine. Maybe we could sit over there, it would be less formal." She nodded toward the small sitting area to the right of the door.

"Please feel free to make yourself comfortable or set up whatever you need while I call them." He moved to the intercom mounted on the wall next to the desk. "Kain, Cody, if you could join us."

"That's handy." She pulled her notebook out of her bag and sat back on the sofa.

"Each of us has our own space to escape to so the intercom makes it easy when we need each other. It's also hooked up in the barn."

"Barn?"

"That's Cody's area mostly. He was raised on a ranch and keeps horses here. In the summer he runs a riding camp for children, and throughout the year he gives underprivileged kids a chance to experience the joys of horses and riding."

"That's sweet. I've never been riding, but I know people who have and they say there's nothing like it." She twirled the pen between her fingers.

"I thought everyone might like a drink." Cody entered carrying a tray. "I wasn't sure what you'd like, this is iced tea but if you prefer something else—"

"Iced tea is fine." She accepted once of the glasses from the tray. "Once Mr. Fitzgerald joins us, we can get started."

"We're on first names here." Aiden took one of the glasses before he sat on the only chair between the two sofas. Kain entered and Aiden turned to him. "I suspect you were doing your normal checks."

Kain looked toward her before he glared at Aiden. "I don't believe this is

30

the time to discuss such things."

She smirked at him. "You can answer his question because I suspect you've been running a background check on me. Without a doubt, you did them on my parents, and most likely completed some checks on all of us, but now that I've shown up instead of my father, you wanted more in-depth checks. Am I right?"

"Least you can do is tell her the truth." Aiden took a sip of his drink.

Kain nodded and lowered himself onto the sofa across from her. "Yes, I did. You didn't honestly expect me to let a stranger into our home without doing the standard checks, no matter whose daughter she may be, did you?"

"Knowing you, no." Aiden leaned back and smirked. "You have the floor now, Paris."

"Thank you." She leaned forward. "Aiden mentioned that you've talked about what you want in a spouse and that's the first step. Now I'd like to know why you chose to go through Beyond Monogamy versus doing this yourself."

"I'll answer that." Kain leaned forward, placing his elbows on his knees. "Sharing a wife was something we decided on years ago. I was raised in a family with two fathers, and because of that, there was always someone there to throw the ball with, to come to my games no matter what sport I played. My mother never seemed happier than when she was with my fathers. It wasn't until I was older that I understood the risks they took. I knew that one day I wanted the same thing my parents had."

"Like Kain, I was raised in a similar family."

She turned to Aiden, confused. "Everything I've read about you shows you were raised in an average family. One mother, one father, a loving environment, strong family ties."

"If you've read that biography then you'll also know my *aunt* lived with us."

The way he stressed *aunt* made her wonder if she'd missed something in her research. "Yes. To help care for you and your mother while your father was traveling for work. I believe I read your mother had breast cancer and passed away a few years ago."

"Yes, but what was kept hidden from the media was my so-called aunt was also my mother. My father was committed to both of them as his wives. Unlike now, they couldn't have an actual wedding joining the three of them, but in their hearts they were married and we were a family."

"Then why was it kept a secret? I mean, I understand why it was kept a secret then because it was illegal, but why now? Why not come out and tell the world?"

"That is my father's secret to tell, not mine." He smiled as if remembering the joys of his childhood. "Though if you've been watching the media, there have been hints that there's a wedding on the horizon for my father. He'll legally marry his second wife in the coming months. It will be a small ceremony for close friends and family. Only those closest to them understand that this is more of a renewal of their vows than an actual wedding."

"I'm the only one who wasn't raised in a family like this." Cody sat on the sofa beside her, his ankle propped on his knee.

"We'll discuss that shortly. Right now, I want all of you to understand how this will work. Today I'm here to gather information about all of you, your wants, needs, dreams, and fears. That will help me determine who the right woman is for you. As I explained to Aiden, this will take time because it's more complicated than most cases."

"Why is this more complicated?" Cody asked, leaning forward.

"Most clients are a married couple searching for an additional partner. Sometimes they are man and wife, other times they're a same sex couple, searching for another. The three of you are not a couple, but you're looking for one to make you complete. That means you haven't already worked out the issues that come with marriage."

"We understand. However long it takes, we know that in the end we'll have the happiness we want. We'll be complete." Aiden nodded.

"We decided on this years ago, but because of my legal career, Aiden and Cody agreed we should wait until we saw how the legal battle your family fought ended. If it had been a bust, we'd have found a way of doing it without making it public," Kain explained. "Which would have been hard for Aiden and myself because our careers are in the forefront of things. But like his parents did, we'd have found a way."

"Aiden is a public figure so it would have been difficult to keep a relationship like this out of the press. There's always publicity of the three of you living together here."

"Oh, we've heard all of that." Cody chuckled.

"Some of the football players I've played with won't come around because they think we're gay. They can't stop thinking about all those years in the locker room…" Aiden trailed off as if he didn't want to think of what had been said by people he had considered friends.

"All three of you need to realize things will only get worse. The media is going to run with the idea of the three of you together, and only advance on it when there's a woman in the mix. They're going to have a field day with this. Do you realize what you're getting yourselves into?"

"Yes." Cody nodded. "We understand the risks but the rewards are more worthwhile. The people who know us will know the truth, and the others can think what they want. We've decided this is what we want and it's time we take steps to achieve it."

"Cody's right." Aiden nodded in agreement. "I understand there might be changes in my career options, but we're financially secure. If I never do that work again, we'll still be fine. Same with Kain, if his legal practice dries up because of this, we're willing to accept that. Right, Kain?"

"Who knows?" Kain smirked. "We could come up with a whole bunch of new clients."

"My father Mathew's career took a hit at first, but now he's working on a high profile murder case." She laid her pen on top of the notebook on her lap.

"I've heard about that. He's prosecuting that woman who killed her daughter while they were on vacation because she couldn't go to the nightclubs at the resort." Cody shook his head, disgusted.

"That's the reason he didn't take Paul's place today and I came instead," she explained.

"Don't you also have a brother who works with the company?"

"Yes." She nodded to Cody before glancing toward Aiden. "I explained to Aiden earlier why he wasn't the one who came. He's too big of a fan to handle business in a professional matter."

"What matters is she's here to help us." Aiden winked at her. "Now instead of questioning why she's here, maybe we could get down to business."

Over the next hour, she went over the process, detailing every step, and answering their questions as they came up. Surprisingly, things went easier than she had expected. They had done their research on most of what would happen. They asked questions about what they were unsure of so there would be no confusions later on.

She had come there unsure her family would be able to help them, but now she had a new lease on what she could do for them. At some point in the midst of the conversation, she had decided she'd find them the wife they had waited so long for. Not only that, but she was determined to find them the *perfect* one. They deserved it. Sometime in the middle of all this, she had warmed up to them. She wanted to help them.

Chapter Four

Aiden stood near the window watching the cows in the pasture. There was a peacefulness to the view, almost relaxing in a way. They weren't their cows, but belonged to the farmer who lived on the adjacent property. It was a deal they had worked out when they purchased the property. He could lease the land, giving his cows more room to roam, in exchange for fresh meat when he butchered an animal or during hunting season. It worked out in their benefit since none of them hunted and the land would have been unused anyway.

"Are you listening to me?" Cody sat perched on the edge of Aiden's desk.

"Yes, I'm listening. What do you want me to say?" He still didn't turn to look at the others, instead he kept his gaze out the window.

"Tell us you feel it too," Cody pushed.

"Cody, you're being too hasty about this. Step back and relax for a minute. She's here on business. Rushing in head-first and screaming she's the one isn't going to make her receptive to the idea." Kain leaned against the wall, watching them.

"What do you expect us to do then? She's leaving in a few hours."

"We need a game plan." Aiden turned from the window to look back at the two men he was closest to, the ones he would spend the rest of his life with. They had become like brothers over the years, knocking sense into his thick head when he was sinking into a deep depression. If it hadn't been for the two of them when his career ended, he wasn't sure what he would've done. Football had been his life, the only real thing he focused on since he was a child, and to have it taken away from him in an instant was devastating.

At least I went out at the end of one of the best games of my life.

He shook his head, chasing away the thoughts of his past and focusing on more important things. It was time to begin building their future with the one woman who would cement them together permanently, and if they had their way, it would be Paris.

"So what's the plan?" Cody slapped his hand down on his leg.

"We're going to meet with her individually like she wants. Answer her questions, but also ask some of our own. We need to know more about her before we can begin convincing her. If we start now she'll think we're nuts, and if she leaves here with that in her mind there's not a chance we'll get her back here. When she leaves, I'll take her back to the plane."

"Aiden, I don't think that's a good idea." Kain pushed off the wall to turn toward him.

"I figured you wouldn't, but you had your time with her and I think I can connect with her on the drive. If anyone has to convince her this is what we want, it's going to be me. She's already mentioned the media coverage."

"They made you look like a player." Cody shook his head. "I told you that you should have come out against that years ago."

"They'd have focused on us." He shrugged his shoulders, as if to convey it was a lose-lose situation. "It wasn't easy, but neither were good options. Being a playboy in the eyes of the media seemed liked a better option at the time than having them hound us day and night trying to catch us in awkward situations."

"It would have been bad either way, but now we're going to have our work cut out for us." Kain took off his cowboy hat and ran this hand through his hair before putting it back on. "I didn't make a very good impression on her when we first met either. I was expecting Mr. Nelson, and when he didn't show I couldn't help but question our decision to work with the company."

"Guess I'm the only one who doesn't have to convince her I'm different than what she thinks." Cody smirked.

Kain shook his head. "You're the youngest and your boyish good looks mean you have to convince her you know what you're doing, including tying yourself to us *and* a woman."

"Why does everyone treat me like I'm a boy?" Cody stretched out his legs.

"Don't knock it, Cody. You have the good looks that will win our woman over. Haven't you noticed how her gaze travels back to you whenever she thinks no one is looking?"

"He's right," Aiden said. "Which is why you're going to talk to her first. Diane will serve the two of you lunch while you're answering whatever questions she has for you. We'll eat in here and whenever you're done Kain will be next. I'm sure she's going to have the most questions for me, therefore it will take more time and maybe she'll be able to eliminate some of the questions after talking to the two of you. I'll meet with her last."

"I'd say you just want to spend all your time with her." Cody stood. "While I'm gone I don't want either of you to worry, I'll smooth the way for you. When I'm done she'll want us as much as we want her."

"Don't lay it on too heavy," Aiden warned while he watched him stroll from the room. Then he turned to Kain. "You know he's going to be overzealous."

"He always is, which is why he works well with us." Kain took a seat in one of the leather chairs across from Aiden's desk. "You know, Paris being the one for us is only going to bring more attention to the situation. Her family is in the center of this new trend, and Beyond Monogamy is getting a lot of attention—both good and bad. It's going to give us twice the media attention."

"I had thought about that, but if she's the one it will be worth it." Aiden sat down behind his desk. "Before my mother died she told me that when the right woman came into my life I'd know it."

"Do you?"

"Yes. I'm not sure I ever believed her, but when I saw Paris walk into my office I knew she was the woman I wanted to spend the rest of my life with. I just hoped you and Cody would feel the same way. Everything else will fall into place, it has to."

His words made him sound so sure, but everything inside of him was turning. He hadn't been this nervous or anxious when he began playing pro-football. Now he sat before one of his best friends wondering how they were going to make this work, because he knew the woman in the other room wasn't going to make things easy for them. There was something about her that screamed she wasn't looking for anything serious, and even if she was it wouldn't be them.

Don't worry, darling, I'm going to convince you otherwise.

Paris stared down at the notebook on the table and wondered why she'd even pulled it out again. It wasn't like she had written anything in it yet. Even when she talked to them as a group, she hadn't added anything to the notebook, but she had no doubt she'd remember it. These guys were going to stick with her long after she found them a wife. The bond was stronger between them than anyone else she'd worked for in the past.

A bond like that is what I want when I marry. She leaned back in her chair and let her thoughts roam. Marriage, commitment, and love were things she wanted, but she had always put finding partners for others above her own needs. There was always a concern she wouldn't find what she was looking for, someone who would understand the family's company meant everything to her. She wouldn't just step away from it, or limit the clients she took on. It wasn't about the fame or the money, what kept her going was the joy she experienced when she saw her matches work out.

That's why she continued her work, even when the publicity was at its worse. The things the media had said about her and the rest of the family stung even if she knew it wasn't true. The people closest to them knew the truth and had ignored the media's comments. She shook her head, not wanting to travel down the road to those memories. She had learned long ago that it wasn't worth getting upset over what they printed about her and the rest of the family.

"Are you ready for me?" Cody stood in the doorway.

"Yes." She nodded to the chair across the table from her. "Please sit."

"Diane will be serving lunch while we talk, if that's okay with you. She's an amazing cook." He took the seat across from her, watching her closely.

"That will be nice, thank you." She sat up straighter in her chair, unsure if she was uneasy because of his penetrating gaze or because of where her thoughts had been before he came into the dining room. "I'll cut straight to it. How old are you, Cody?"

"Your research didn't tell you that?" He raised an eyebrow. "You can't honestly expect me to believe you didn't do the background checks on all of us just as Kain did when you arrived."

"I know what the file says but I want to hear it from you."

"Thirty-two." He paused as Diane placed lunch on the table.

"Burgundy wine chicken breast marinated and served over fresh vegetables," she said, her voice soft and melodic. "I hope you enjoy."

"It looks delicious. Thank you." Paris smiled at Diane before the older woman scurried back to the kitchen.

"Can we get back to my age since you seem to have an issue with it?"

"I asked your age because I wasn't sure I could believe the number in my file. You look younger and I wanted to make sure."

"So, because I look young you think I don't know what I'm getting myself into?" He took a bite of the chicken, his gaze fixed on her.

"Aiden is thirty-five and Kain thirty-six, I just want to make sure you're ready for what you're getting yourself into. A relationship like this can be harder at times, more problems when starting out. You're not just working with one person and dealing with their needs or wants. Instead there's going to be four of you working together, and that will cause more problems until each of you learn to handle it."

"Aiden, Kain, and I already know that. We've lived together long enough to have worked out some of these issues. I understand that by adding another person into the mix, especially a woman, a whole new set of problems could develop. Haven't you ever wanted something you just knew was right? That's how all of us feel about this." He sat his fork aside and leaned forward. "We're not doing this because it's the popular thing. We are doing this because it's what we believe in, what we want."

"You said why the three of you are doing it but why are you personally interested in this? You could have any woman you wanted, why would you want to share one with two others that you have no sexual relations with?"

"That's a good question." He took another bite of his lunch before answering. "My father died when I was young, leaving my mother and me alone. I had just turned sixteen and suddenly I was the man of the house. I gave up sports and everything else to take over the ranch. I was up before the sun, did the chores before school, then after school I rushed home to finish what I didn't get done that morning. There was no time for anything else. I barely graduated because I was too exhausted to deal with school after working on the ranch all evening. I'd fall into bed and sleep like the dead until my alarm went off."

When he paused, she stopped mid-bite and looked at him. "I'm not sure that answers my question."

"If it hadn't been for my mother's health and then Aiden's job offer, I'd have kept the ranch. Now I have a little piece of it here with me. The horses, the riding school, and the work I do with the underprivileged children in the area." He paused and took a drink of the iced tea Diane had brought out earlier. "If something happened to me, I don't want to leave my children and wife alone. I want them to have people like Aiden and Kain. They might not have the interest in the horses, and that's fine, they could close up shop or hire a ranch hand. What is important is that there's someone there for my wife and children. Unlike when it was Mom and me, we were alone. I don't want that so that's one of the reasons I chose this."

"One of the reasons?"

"I knew you'd ask about that the moment I said it." He smirked. "I've seen Kain's family. The love he has for both of his fathers and his mother. There's also a strong connection between each of the parents that I want to have. Aiden's mother died before I came into the picture but I've heard of the joys he had growing up with his two mothers and father. That's the family I want my children raised in."

"Family seems important to you."

"It is. I want a few children. At least one of each but I'll take what my wife will give me and what we're blessed with."

"Have the three of you discussed children? Do the others feel the same way about having them?" She cut more of the chicken into bite size pieces while she watched the joy of the idea of children spread across his face.

"That was covered and we all want kids. Each of us have our own strengths, so we want to teach our children what we know and believe in. I think that will give them a stronger upbringing than I ever had."

She took another bite of chicken before setting her fork aside. "I'd say there was nothing better than growing up with three parents. I spent most of my time with Mom in the kitchen, but London was always out with one of our dads throwing the ball around. I got plenty of attention from my dads. I just never had much interest in sports. Instead, they taught me self-defense, gun

41

safety, and martial arts. Things I could use to protect myself and in the end that was more valuable than learning to throw a baseball."

"Oh, a girl who can take care of herself, I like that." He wiggled his eyebrows at her. "Is that why you're without guards?"

"Why would you think I travel with guards?" She tried to brush it off without going into details, but the smirk on his face told her it wouldn't be that easy.

"We've all done our research and I know your family has received death threats. Last week there was an attack at Mathew's law office. Are you really going to try to tell me you don't have a group of your own guards?"

"You're right, I do, but they didn't come on this journey. Only Jake—our pilot who's waiting for me at the jet—and I made this trip due to the delicate nature of this situation. As I told Kain on our way here, I'm not some helpless woman. I can take care of myself if it comes to it." She took a drink of her tea and tried to regain her control of the situation. She was supposed to be questioning him, not the other way around. "Since one of you were supposed to pick me up at the landing strip, and when I return home my guards will be waiting there to make sure I make it safely home, there was nothing to worry about."

"If you say so." He shrugged and popped a piece of broccoli into his mouth.

"How did you know about the attack at the law office? We kept that very quiet and it never made the news."

"Aiden has his ways, but you'd have to ask him about them. I just heard about the attack when we were discussing the company and your father. Were they able to determine if it was based on the case he's working on, or because of his stance on this lifestyle?"

She pushed her plate aside. No matter how delicious the food was, she'd suddenly lost her appetite. The attack on her father's law office had shaken the family to the core. They had known it was dangerous for them before, but this had brought it home because one of their close friends suffered burns on his arms and chest from being in the way when the Molotov cocktail was thrown through the window.

"I'm sorry, I didn't think before—"

She held up a hand to stop him. "There's nothing to apologize for. If you're concerned that having Beyond Monogamy find you a match will bring danger to yourself and the others, I can't put your mind at ease. The laws are still new and people are still fighting or protesting them. Some of them might take more physical actions to anyone known to be committed to more than one person. That is something all three of you need to consider."

"That's not why I asked." He leaned forward, placing his hands on the table. "I asked because I care if people are putting you and your loved ones in harm's way. No one deserves to live in fear, no matter how they choose to live their life."

"It's been a part of my life for so long I don't know if I remember how to live without being on constant guard. The only time I feel completely safe is when I'm home because it's like a fortress and there's little chance anyone could penetrate it without inside help. The guards we've hired add an additional layer of security."

"Aiden has had his share of irate fans but our home has never been a prison. We've never had to live with the constant fear your family does, and we've never had to have bodyguards follow us when we go out. Due to some issues, we prefer that Aiden doesn't leave our home alone often, but that's for his safety. Once this comes out it could be more dangerous for him but we'll take our chances."

"Irate fans? What kind of danger is Aiden in? Has he received threats from people?"

"There have been threats, minor to extreme, but no attempts on our home or his life if that's what you're concerned about." He paused as Diane cleaned up their plates before continuing. "There are fans who haven't been too happy that he's retired, others who disagree with his business decisions. In life, you can't please everyone so it's best to do what's right for you. He's done just that."

She nodded and decided it was time to steer the conversation back on track so she could get to the other two and back to the plane before nightfall. "That's good advice, and something you should remember once I find you a spouse. The four of you are going to have to work together and be damned if you let the world stop you."

Coming into this meeting with Cody, he had been the one she was the most unsure about. His appearance made him seem younger than the others, and she had worries that they might be leading him into something *they* wanted without considering his feelings. For a relationship like this to work, it had to be something they all wanted and it appeared she had him all wrong.

She'd thought he was the one who would want it the least, but his reasons for wanting this relationship to work were the strongest. First impressions weren't always right and he had proven that. Actually, they were all proving it.

Chapter Five

Aiden had tried to busy himself with the work that needed his attention, investment decisions Kain was waiting for and other busy work, but his thoughts were on Paris. He hadn't expected the woman they'd been waiting for to walk through his front door, but there was an instant connection between them he wouldn't have believed possible if he hadn't felt it within every cell of his body.

He glanced at the picture of his parents that sat in the center of his desk. They were there guiding him even if they weren't close enough to pop in whenever he needed someone to talk to. Both of his mothers would be proud of how everything was working out. Thinking of them had him reaching for his cell phone; he needed to hear the reassuring voices of his parents. He was a grown man, on his own for more years than he cared to count, but his parents were still a huge part of his life.

He scrolled down the list of contacts on his cell phone until he reached his parents' number and hit the call button. He brought his cell phone to his ear just in time to hear his father's rough voice as he answered.

"Hi, Dad, got a minute?"

"I've always got a minute for you, son. The interview with Mr. Nelson not going well?" He could hear his father shut the table saw off, which meant he

45

was out in his workshop doing another project. Last time they spoke, it had been new cabinets for the house.

"It's not with Mr. Nelson, but his daughter Paris."

"Ahh. That pretty brunette. Is she impossible to work with?"

Aiden turned the chair until he could look out the windows that spanned behind him and to one side of him, affording a grand view because his office was situated on the corner of the house. "Just the opposite, Dad. When you met your wives, did you know they were the ones?"

"I thought you weren't paying attention when Mom told you that you'd recognize the people you were destined to spend your life with. You were young and wanted nothing to do with serious relationships, let alone marriage, all you wanted to focus on was football."

"So you knew when you met both my moms?" He pushed, wanting a more direct answer.

"With Christine, I knew immediately. I walked into her father's hardware store and the moment your mother turned around to see if I needed help finding anything, I was gone. She tucked a strand of her blonde hair behind her ear and our eyes met. There was an instant connection. One that was there every day, and even now…though she's not here with us, sometimes I swear I can feel her presence." Charlie paused for a moment and Aiden gave him time to enjoy those memories. "Don't get me wrong, son, she never made it easy for me. Not one single day, but I loved that woman."

Aiden's second mother, Susan, had confided in him that his father blamed himself for Christine's death. Aiden didn't want him to ruminate on it. "What about with Susan? Was it the same way?"

"I was attracted to Susan, but it was your mother who pushed me. She knew our family needed something more and she was right. Susan completed us." There was a pause. "What's this about?"

"I think we've found her." He didn't need to go into details. His father

46

already knew the three men were looking for a woman to spend their lives with. Neither of his parents even batted an eyelash when he'd told them. It was actually the opposite. His father asked why it took them so long to come out with something he'd suspected long ago.

"Good for you, son. Who is she?"

Aiden rested his head against the back of the leather chair and let his eyes drift shut until he conjured her image in his mind. "Paris Nelson."

"She's a beautiful young woman but there's a danger level surrounding her because of her family's part in the legal battle for this lifestyle. You have to realize you and the others will be targets as well."

"Just as you and Mom will be," Aiden reasoned.

"Don't worry about us. We want you happy, and you know Mom would have both of our asses if you didn't follow your heart for fear of what danger might come to us. Now instead of talking to me, you should be telling her this."

"Dad, it's not that simple." He ran a hand through his hair. "How do I tell her that she's the one? She came here for business, nothing more."

"Well, don't rush in like a bull in a china shop. Take things slow and everything will fall into place."

"Hey." Kain stood in the doorway. "She's ready for you."

"Tell her I'll be right there." Aiden turned his attention back to the phone. "Dad, I should go. She's waiting for me."

"Go, and good luck. Remember things will fall into place." His father gave a light laugh before adding, "It's going to be fine. We love you, son."

"Love you too, Dad." He ended the call and turned to Kain. "How did it go?"

"She's more relaxed than she was. Cody seemed to have softened her some, which worked for me, and allowed me to make amends for earlier. Now it's your chance to go in there and sweep her off her feet. I'm assuming you were talking to Charlie. Did he give you the kick in the ass you need to get the job done? We're all counting on you."

"No pressure." Aiden stood and came around the desk. "Dad said it will all fall into place, but I'll do my best. I don't know what you expect, it's not like she's just going to drop everything and stay here."

"No, but it will give her something to consider when she's flying home tonight. Maybe she'll come back and we won't have to go to her to convince her. There's no need for her to use valuable hours searching for a wife for us if we've already found her," Kain reasoned as he leaned against the door frame.

"I'll do what I can." He strolled past Kain and headed toward the dining room where she waited.

He knew she wouldn't stay, but it was what he wanted. He wanted her close so they could begin to learn about each other, explore one anothers wants and needs, and eventually explore each others bodies. He wanted to start their lives together, not let her get back on that plane and fly back home.

The soles of his dress shoes clicked against the hardwood floors as he made his way closer to her. With each step, he knew he was nearing his destiny and the woman he was meant to be with. He drew a deep breath and turned the corner to enter the dining room. "Are you ready for me?"

Paris looked up from the notebook she was writing in, turning her beautiful hazel eyes to him. "Yes, Mr. Dalton, please have a seat."

"I thought we were past the *Mr.* phase. Please call me Aiden." He took a seat across from her.

"Aiden." She gave him the brightest smile he'd seen on her since she arrived. "When my father asked me to come, I was pretty sure we wouldn't be able to help you. I was convinced the media was right in how they portrayed you. However, in the last few hours you have convinced me what was done to you was the same thing that happened to my family. The media portrayed us as monsters, there were even articles claiming we were abused because of the life my parents chose…but I'm straying from the point."

"What is your point?"

"I believe Beyond Monogamy can help you find a wife. When I return home, I'll search our available women and determine the best matches for you. I'll return in a week or two and go over the ones that I think might be the best for the three of you, and we can go from there."

He bit the inside of his cheek to keep from announcing they already found the woman they wanted. Instead, he leaned forward, placed his hands on the table, and looked her directly in the eyes. "When you were given our file what did you actually think? That I was a playboy?"

Her cheeks turned red with embarrassment, which he found completely adorable, before she forced herself to look away. "That's not the point."

"I want to know."

"The media portrayed you as a playboy, going out with different women all the time. When I found out it was you…" She paused, wringing her hands.

"Go on. I promise not to hold it against you or the company." He smirked. He had to admit to himself that he was enjoying her moment of discomfort, but that wasn't the reason he'd pressed her to continue. No, he needed to know so he could find out if her opinion of him had changed. If not, he might have to work harder to convince her.

"I wanted to know how many wives you wanted," she blurted out before closing her notebook. "Now that you know what I thought of you, should I assume you will be going with another company?"

He reached over the wide custom table that extended across the length of the dining room, and cupped his hand over hers. Soft cool flesh met his warm fingers and he had the desire to rub his hands over hers until they were warm. "I told you I wouldn't hold it against you or the company, and I'm a man of my word."

"You're still going to use Beyond Monogamy?" The surprise was thick in her voice.

"Tell me, has your opinion of me changed? Or do you still think I'm a playboy?"

She shook her head, sending her honey brown hair slipping gently around her face. He wanted to run his fingers through it, nudge it away from her eyes. "No. I already said you and the others changed my mind. If I still had the same impression of you, I wouldn't be willing to help you."

"So you don't think I'm a chauvinistic pig, at least that's one good thing." He leaned back against the chair. "Clubbing was never my scene, but my agent demanded that I go out. I had an image to uphold, promotional agreements that forced me to attend certain events, and club openings I had to go to. None of it was my idea, but…"

"It was your career," she supplied. "I understand that, but before I came here I thought it must also be a part of you or you wouldn't be doing it."

"Sometimes in life we have to do things we don't like. Then there are times we find something or someone we didn't expect, and we have to hold onto it with both hands."

"I'm hoping I can find the one you're looking for quickly."

"Sometimes people are brought together for different reasons and instead they find love. I have no doubt everything is going to work out just fine." He dropped the first hint of what he was thinking before quickly changing the subject. He wanted to plant the idea without giving her too much time to consider it. "I thought you had questions for me."

As if remembering she was here on business, she picked up her pen again and looked down at her notebook. "The others answered a lot of my general questions. The biggest question I have now is what do you want and need in a wife? What are you looking for in the woman you're going to spend the rest of your life with?"

Over the next twenty minutes, he answered her questions, going into details about what he wanted. It wasn't like he had a list of demands, but he wanted a wife who would understand there were still threats upon his life because of his business transactions. He didn't want someone who was so headstrong they wouldn't take the precautions his life demanded. That was one of the reasons she was a perfect fit; she already understood the need to take steps to remain safe.

As they talked, he was able to learn a little more about her. Not as much as he'd like, but enough to know she was completely dedicated to her family's company. She needed to get out of the office, enjoy life. She spent all her time helping others find a happy-ever-after, but was neglecting herself. He was determined to see that things changed there. Work was just that; it shouldn't consume her life completely.

"Those are all the questions I have for you. Whenever Kain is ready I'll be on my way." She closed her notebook and slipped it into her laptop bag.

"Actually, I'm going to drive you back to the plane." He watched as she paused, and he wondered why she hesitated. "Does that bother you?"

"I just assumed you'd have other things to attend to, that's all." She stood and lifted her bag on her shoulder. "I'm ready then."

"I'd like to show you something before we leave." He came around the table and nodded to the door. "It won't take long."

He guided her out of the room with his hand on the small of her back, then led her down the hall and toward the far staircase. He wanted to show her the lookout room. It was the one place in the house with views that went on for miles. The house was everything he wanted and so much more, but this room was more than just a room. It had become a sanctuary for him, a place where he organized his thoughts, where he escaped the stress of his work. He hoped taking her to see a place that was special to him would make her realize there was more to life than just work. It was something Cody and Kain had shown him years ago, and now he was going to do the same with her.

"Where are we going?"

Her question invaded his thoughts, forcing his attention back on her. "Upstairs."

"For what?" She stopped in her tracks, refusing to move as he tried to lead her forward. "Mr. Dalton—"

"*Aiden*, please…and there's something I want to show you before you leave. It's completely innocent, and before you start wondering it's not a bedroom." He smirked as images of taking her to his bedroom played through his head, and his shaft began to respond to the fantasies. "Down the hall to the back staircase, and up two flights of steps. I promise when you get up there all will be revealed, and it will be worth the few minutes. Trust me."

"Okay, but then I should get back to the plane."

"Directly after, I'll take you there." He let her go in front of him as they began to climb the stairs for his own selfish reasons; he wanted to watch her ass move. With every step he wanted to reach out and touch it, or her in general.

This woman was already working her way into every thought he had. He hadn't been able to focus on work. Since she arrived, he had been focused on how he was going to convince her they no longer needed her matchmaking services because she was the one. His father's advice that everything would fall into place might be good, but the three of them needed to put a plan together on how they were going to approach this. They needed to work together to claim their woman.

"Aiden," she called, waving her hand in front of his face.

He shook his head, sending his thoughts floating away as if on water. Now with his head clear, he realized she had said something. "Sorry, what?"

"I asked you where we were going now."

"Through that door." He nodded to the second door. "The other is the bathroom. It connects to where we're going, but also has a door from the hall. This area could be used as another master bedroom, but all three of us have our space on the second floor so this isn't set up that way. Open the door and find out what's there."

She did as he asked and they stepped into a large room with floor to ceiling windows that showed off every aspect of the view three different ways. The only wall that was closed off was to the bathroom, but with the house backed up against a mountain, the view wasn't lacking anything on that side. The furniture was minimal in here. Two warm brown sofas were positioned so one could take advantage of the views, and there was no television or any other diversion. This place was for relaxation. When any of the guys came up here, they left their cell phones downstairs, and the others knew not to bother them unless it was an emergency. This was the one place they could just be and not have to worry about daily stresses.

"It's beautiful." She moved closer to the windows while he hung back, giving her a moment to enjoy it. "It looks like the land just goes on and on."

"The room was Cody's idea. He's always been more in touch with the land and outdoors than the rest of us."

"It's a view to be envious of that's for sure. The gentle rolling hills, green grass, animals roaming…and then in the distances the mountains shooting up like giant stairways to the sky." She spun around to see the view from the other side. "No matter what way you look it's stunning."

"Whether the sun is rising or setting, you can see it from here. Maybe on your next visit you'll be sure to time it for the sunset. It is really something you shouldn't miss. It's a truly unforgettable experience." One he wanted to experience with her. To see the last rays of sunshine off her body, mixing with the warm orange, pink, and blue tones, was something he didn't want to miss.

She nodded but didn't give him an answer. "My home office has the view of the mountains but nothing like this. I can see the snow covered peaks, but that's about it because of the high walls that have been built surrounding our property. It keeps us safe but it obstructs the views. Whereas this…this is just amazing."

He came to stand next to her, and when she looked at him, there was a twinkle of happiness in her eyes. The others might have wondered why he brought her somewhere that was so special to them. This was their private area, one they never allowed visitors to venture in. But this was all part of his plan. She'd leave and this spot would be on her mind; he hoped it would lead her thoughts back to them. Her next visit would be scheduled for later in the day, and she could enjoy a romantic sunset with them—one they'd be ready for.

Chapter Six

The house was eerily quiet as Paris made her way toward London's office in search of an update on Mom's condition. She had planned to see her parents, but with the silence, she thought her mother might be resting and didn't want to disturb them. With the cancer treatments taking a toll on Mom, she wouldn't disturb them if they had finally managed to get some sleep.

"Paris," London whispered from the middle of the staircase leading upstairs.

"Why are you whispering?" She kept her voice low to match his but all she got was a gesture asking her to climb the steps before he turned and started walking. Seeking answers, she followed him, climbing the stairs two at a time before finding him on the landing between their spaces. His bedroom, office, and sitting room were to the left while hers were to the right. "What the hell's going on?"

"The treatment was rough today and Mom's resting."

Now that she was closer, she could see the strain around his eyes. For the first time she saw something in him she hadn't seen before. Fear. He was growing up and facing things head on like the rest of them had to, instead of hiding behind partying or work. "Dads?"

"Paul is with her and Mathew has gone to get a new medication the doctor prescribed." He rubbed a hand over his face before looking at her again. "I've never seen her this bad. I feel so helpless, there's nothing any of us can do."

She reached toward him, laying her hand on his arm. "We can be there for her. We can deal with the company so Dads can be by her side during the treatments and when she's here. They'll let us know if there's anything else we can do. Otherwise, as hard as it is, we just have to wait. Mom's strong, she'll get through this."

"I hope so. I know they don't want us to worry but when you see the worry in our fathers' eyes, it's hard not to. Mathew has been putting in fewer hours at the office and working more from home. I thought at first it was because of the attack on the office, but now I realize he wants to be close to Mom."

"Even Mathew has been doing less and clinging to Mom more."

"Do you think they know something we don't? Could they have given Mom a time frame?"

She ran her hand up his arm, chasing away the goosebumps that had risen on his skin. "We can't think like that. I don't believe our parents would keep something like that from us, and the doctors wouldn't be pushing such a high radiation and chemotherapy round on her, three days a week, if they didn't believe there was a chance it would send her back into remission."

"Mom is the center of this family, the one who keeps us all together. What happens if she doesn't make it?"

"She's going to and we're not going to think like this." She nodded to her door. "Why don't you come in and have a drink with me?"

"I can't, I've got an early flight to Florida. Can I have a rain check?"

"Sure, when you get back. I thought Jake was off tomorrow."

"He is." He raised his eyebrows at her, giving her a wide-eyed expression. "The horror, but I have to travel like common folk. This was a last minute trip. I don't know if you remember Mr. Langer and his family, but his second wife was killed in a car accident last night. I'm going to attend the funeral and see if there's anything I can do to help them."

"I remember them. He hired us to find him a third wife."

He nodded. "Wonder if that makes her the second wife now."

"Anything you need me to cover while you're gone?"

"I've got most everything done, and Dottie will handle the rest. If anything comes up I'll let you know because I'm not sure how long I'll be there." He turned his sparkling blue eyes toward her—his father Paul's eyes. "Paris…you will call me if anything changes with Mom, right? I can get the first plane back."

"You know I will and I'll send Jake to fetch you if you can't get a flight home. It's going to be okay."

He nodded and turned back toward his open door, but she could tell she hadn't been able to relieve his worry. That didn't surprise her because she was terrified they'd lose Mom, too. "London." She waited until he looked over his shoulder toward her. "I love you, little brother."

"Love you too, sis." He stepped into his quarters and closed the door, leaving her standing in the hall alone.

She needed to know how Mom was but didn't want to disturb Paul. Instead, she pulled her cell phone out of her bag as she headed to her room and pulled up Mathew's cell number. She sent him a quick text message asking him to stop by her room when he got home. With that done, she pushed the door shut to change out of her business suit and into something more comfortable before checking her email and voice messages.

She quickly slipped out of her clothes and into a pair of heather gray yoga pants and a white tank top before heading toward her desk. Even after the long day, there were things she wanted to attend to. Most likely phone calls from clients she had to return, and she knew there were emails that required her attention. On the airplane she could have pulled out her laptop and worked but her thoughts were preoccupied with Aiden. Well, not just him, but all three of them. She couldn't separate herself from his case as she had done in the past with other clients.

She pulled her laptop from her bag, sat it on the desk, and booted it up. It was too late to make the calls she needed to some clients, but she could reply to the emails. More importantly, she wanted to start the system running a detailed check on all three of the men. She wanted to eliminate any surprises they'd failed to mention during her visit before she went any further. Maybe she'd find something that would force her to push them from her thoughts. She was beginning to think they were perfect for *her*.

She shook her head, trying to chase that thought away. She was their matchmaker, and that was as far as things would go. There was no use wondering how their hands would feel on her body. Or worse yet, what it would be like to have them in her bed.

They were attractive, but it was more than that for her. These men had answered questions about what was important to them just as she would have. When matching people, they were matched on levels beyond physical compatibilities. They needed to want the same things, have the same goals, desires, and so much more. If she was the client and not the matchmaker, she'd have thought they'd be a perfect fit for each other.

"Damn it, Paris, no!" She scolded herself just as there was a knock at her door. "Come in."

Mathew peaked around the corner. "Hey, sweetie, I got your text."

"Come in, Dad." When he hesitated, she added, "It'll only take a minute and then you can get back to Mom."

He entered, closed the door behind him, and came closer to her desk. "Thanks for covering the Aiden Dalton case for Paul. Did you have a good trip?"

"It was fine and I promised to find them the perfect wife, so don't worry about that. You and Dad need to focus on Mom. The case isn't why I asked you to come up here." She strolled around the desk, standing closer to him.

"How is she? Truthfully, Dad."

"My sweet little girl is all grown up." He smiled at her but there was a sadness in his eyes.

"I'll always be your little girl, Dad, but I need the truth. How bad is the cancer this time?"

He laid the brown bag from the drugstore on the desk and sat down on the only chair in front of her desk. "Oh, Paris."

She knelt in front of him, taking his hands in hers. "That bad?"

"It's worse than last time, and you know how hard that was on her. This chemo and radiation combination was a killer, and today was only the first day. It's going to get worse over the next three weeks. Three treatments each week for the next three weeks before her doctors want to run a fresh batch of tests, but it's possible there'll be an additional three weeks."

Three to six weeks of this combination therapy might be Hell, but if it kept Mom here, they all knew they'd fight to make it happen. Mom wasn't a quitter, none of them were. She pushed back the tears that threatened to fall. "Mom's strong and we're going to get through this. What can I do to help?"

"You're already doing too much."

"Dad, we're family and we're there for each other. London and I have the company managed, but what else can I do?" She ran her thumb over his knuckles.

"There's nothing you can do. Not really." He paused, glancing from her desk and back to her. "Just spend time with her when she's up to it. If this has taught me one thing, it's we never know when our days are over."

"She's not—" She couldn't bring herself to give him false hope, because in the end no one knew when their time was over. "Dad, there hasn't been a time line given, has there?"

He turned from her and refused to meet her gaze. "I've got to get back to them."

"Dad!" She didn't budge when he started to get up. If he wanted to stand, he'd have to push her out of the way. "If anything has been said like that I've got a right to know. London and I have a right to know so we can cherish whatever time she has left."

"Paris." He finally looked at her, and she saw terror in his eyes. He was scared of losing his wife. "The doctor didn't say it to your mother, he's a friend of Paul's and he mentioned it, but there's nothing definite."

"What did he say?" Despite the fact it was going to break her heart, she still needed to know.

"He only mentioned that if this treatment combination doesn't work, it's our last hope. That…" His voice broke before he was able to continue. "That we needed to prepare for the possibility…that she wouldn't make it to the first thaw."

Deflated, she sank back on her heels. The possibility that her mother's cancer wouldn't go into remission again had hung over them, a constant fear since the news came that the cancer was back with a vengeance. But the first thaw? It was January, that didn't leave much time. She couldn't stop the tears from rolling down her face.

"Paul and I made the decision not to tell you or London until we knew something definite. There's no reason to worry if this treatment works. If not, we'll know in three weeks and then we would have told you."

"It's that bad." The words came out barely above a whisper.

"I'm afraid so, sweetie." He stood, drawing her into his arms and held her tight as she cried. She wasn't sure how long he held her, but when she finally pulled away he added, "Let's keep this to ourselves, don't tell London yet. He's already worried about Mom and there's no reason to stress him out more until we know something."

"I think he already suspects something. When I came home tonight, he was waiting for me. He's worried about her. I know we all are, but I still think he should know before he leaves for Florida in the morning. As you said, no one knows what the future holds. None of us will ever forgive ourselves if he gets on that plane tomorrow and something happens to her."

He shook his head. "I'm leaving here at six in the morning and you know he's not an early riser. It's going to have to wait until he gets back because I'm not going to ask Paul to watch for London in the midst of caring for Mom."

"I'll do it."

"You've had a long day and I'm sure you have work you need to attend to. He'll be back in a few days."

"No, Dad. He needs to know. I'll tell him in the morning if that's okay with you."

He took a deep breath and exhaled before nodding. "Tell him not to say anything to Mom. We don't want her to know or to give up fighting. If she becomes discouraged, we might lose her."

"I'll make it clear, but if there's anything I can do please come to me."

"I will, but now I have to get back to Mom. I love you, sweetie." He kissed her cheek before reaching past her to grab the drugstore bag.

"I love you too, Dad. Give Mom and Dad my love too."

When he left, she leaned against her desk. The work she had planned to do was suddenly unimportant. It was as if her whole world had shattered around her. Before she spoke to London, she needed to get her head together. Her emotions were all over the place, making logical thought nearly impossible.

Needing fresh air, she pulled open the sliding door to her private balcony and stepped outside. The cold winter air enveloped her, welcoming her to the winter wonderland. Below her, she saw the guard making his patrol of the perimeter. Everyone around her was going about their business, while she tried to face the eventual death of her mother. She was only twenty-five and London twenty-three; they were both adults, but they should have their mother around for many more years to come. Mom should be able to see her children get married, have children of their own, and enjoy all the other milestones of the future.

Standing there in the cold, she let the tears fall until her body shook. She gave herself time alone to fall apart so she could put the pieces together and be strong for her family. By the time the tears had ended, she was shivering from the cold. Her cell phone, which she forgot she'd shoved into the waistband of her yoga pants, was vibrating. She tugged it out with the intention of sending whoever was calling straight to voicemail. Aiden Dalton's name on the screen caught her attention, and without thinking, she answered and brought it to her ear.

"Hello, Mr. Dalton." She couldn't bring herself to answer more formally, and ask him what she could do for him, because at the moment she just wanted to hear his voice. *Damn it, Paris. He's not yours. Don't get attached.*

"Is everything okay?"

"I don't believe you called to see if I was fine. What can I do for you?" She quickly avoided the question, while her mind screamed for her to tell him. She wanted to hear someone tell her it would be okay, even if it was a lie.

"You're right. I didn't, but the sound of your voice tells me something is wrong. Trust me, when you travel away from your family for years you tend to pick up on things like the changes in someone's voice. Are you okay, Paris?"

"Just a little bad news." She shook her head. That was the understatement of the year. "Nothing to worry about. If you're calling to see how the matchmaking is going, it's too early."

"No." He let out a light laugh. "I guess you've had people call the same day wondering about a match."

"A few." She stared out at the mountains, wishing she was skiing down one of them. "I just got home, but I'll get started in the morning and will be in touch soon." *After one last deeper background check is complete on all three of you.*

"That's not why I called. The guys and I were talking after you left, and we

62

think in order for you to find a perfect wife for us, you need to come back."

"I've gathered the answers I need for the search." She pushed the sliding glass door open and stepped inside. Immediately the heat began to warm her and she was able to focus. "There's no need for another visit at this stage."

"This upcoming Saturday we're having an informal family get together with my parents and Kain's parents. I think if you met our families, because they're the people we're closest to, it will give you another insight on what we need in a spouse."

"Mr. Dalton…Aiden, I'm not sure I'm available this weekend."

"I understand you have other clients and commitments, but I think it will give you a better idea of us. A different side of each of us you couldn't see in an interview."

"It's been a long day." She rolled her shoulders. "Can I get back to you tomorrow? Once I check my planner and talk to my family. With London going out of town tomorrow I need to make sure things are covered here."

"Very well." He paused and she heard his desk chair creak forward. Instantly her thoughts were filled with him behind the grand desk, the pastures, and mountains in the background, before her imagination took a more erotic turn, his voice pulled her back. "There are rumors that your mother is sick again."

She stayed quiet. The family had decided to keep the fact that her mother's cancer had returned quiet. They didn't want anyone focused on that, especially not with Mathew currently prosecuting the woman who killed her own daughter while on vacation.

"Shall I take your silence as an admission?"

"Mr. Dalton, my family business is just that, my business." She knew she couldn't afford to be snippy with this client but she needed to set up boundaries.

"Very well. I'll give you a call tomorrow night and see if you will grace our gathering with your presence. Until then, Paris, I hope your dreams are full of wonders of the future." With that, he clicked off, not giving her time to say goodbye or anything else.

She stood there holding the phone, wondering why she didn't agree to the family gathering. At least then she'd be closer to him and the others, even if it was only for a short time before she matched them. Soon her time with them would be over and she'd be able to get back to her normal life and try to forget them. *You'll never be able to forget them.*

Chapter Seven

The dark and threatening sky matched Paris's mood. She sat behind her desk, the work piling up, but she couldn't keep her thoughts on anything. How did one deal with knowing death's long fingers were closing in for the kill? If she could discover the answer for that, she might be able to get back to the things that needed to be completed by the end of the day.

London had taken the news as she expected he would and hadn't wanted to catch his plane. After countless promises to call him and send Jake for him if anything happened, she had managed to get him out the door and on his way. Now that he was gone she half wished he'd stayed. There was nothing he could have done but at least she'd have someone to talk to, to confide in. Her dads were too busy caring for Mom and didn't need to be bothered by her fears.

"Busy?" Paul stood in the door frame in the jeans and t-shirt he favored when he was around the house.

"Not really. What's up?" She tried to keep her tone light and not let her emotions show through.

"Mom wants to see you."

"How is she?" She laid her pen aside and pushed her chair back.

"Tired but at least she's been able to eat something this morning. Tomorrow she has another round of treatment so if you can come down to see her today while she's feeling better that would be good."

"I'll go now." She stood and came around the desk, closer to him.

"Mathew told you about what the doctor said, but remember she doesn't know."

"I won't say anything, Dad. I also know we need to keep things upbeat for her and not stress her out. This hasn't been the first time we've been through this." She forced herself to smile because she was going to have to when she got downstairs.

"This time it's harder." The sadness leaked through his voice.

She nodded. "I know, Dad, I know."

"You go ahead and see her, I need to get a little air." He strolled from her office before she could say anything.

As she headed downstairs to her parents' room, she realized this cancer was taking a toll on all of them. No matter what anyone said, when someone in the family was fighting a battle against cancer the whole family fought. Everyone had to be strong, supportive, and pick up the slack for the others. Their family had always been tight knit, but this had brought them even closer.

She came to stand in front of the double doors leading to the first floor master suite that was her parents' bedroom, took a deep breath and pushed the thoughts of losing her mother from her mind. This was no time to give in to the loss of not only her mother but also her best friend. She had to be brave. With her emotions in check, she knocked lightly on the door and pushed it open. "Mom."

"Come sit with me." Her mother, Amy, patted the bed next to her.

"Mom." Her voice cracked before she pulled a tight rein on her emotions again.

"I'm fine, sweetie. Now I want to talk to you about these new clients."

She came to sit next to her mother and took her hand in hers. "You three shouldn't be worrying about the company, London and I have everything under control."

"I'm not worried about it. I know you're a perfectionist and won't give up until everything is just right. Child, you work too hard." She squeezed Paris's hand. "I heard you're working with Aiden Dalton, and I just want you to know that if he's too...*grabby* or anything, I want you to turn it down. We don't need clients like that. I don't care what your fathers say about what it will do for the business, I won't have you working with people like that."

"Oh, Mom, he's not like that at all." She couldn't keep the smile from spreading across her face. "He's so sweet, and nothing like what the media made him out to be. He's kind and attentive. Kain and Cody are just as great."

"Child, is there something you want to tell me?"

She had planned to keep her attraction to Aiden, Kain, and Cody a secret, but she wanted the intimate moment with her mother. "With every question they answered, I felt drawn to them. They were answering just as I'd want the man...men...I spend my life with to answer."

"Then why are you here? You should be there, getting to know them. Maybe you're the right person for them."

"Mom—"

"Paris, don't you sit there and tell me you're here because of my treatments. I'm going to be fine, I don't give a shit what the doctor said." Paris stilled under her mother's hand. "Don't think I don't know what they said."

"What are you talking about?" She tried to act as if she didn't know. Maybe her mother was talking about something other than the timeframe the doctor mentioned to Paul.

"Daughter of mine, we're too much alike. You can't lie very well. I know the doctor said I wouldn't live through winter if this treatment doesn't work."

"But how?"

"Doctor Vander stood in this very house and said it. Paul thought I was resting and Mathew was working, but I was hungry and went to get something to eat. They were standing in the foyer when Doctor Vander stopped by to pick up the dish his wife used to bring food over when she heard my cancer had returned." Amy moved farther up in bed so she was sitting and leaned against the pillows. "I'm not stupid, I knew the cancer was worse this time, but I'm not going to let it beat me."

"Oh, Mom, why didn't you tell us you knew?"

"I've tried to approach the subject with Paul but he shuts me down before I can tell him, and Mathew's got his mind on the case. When I see him, I want to *just* be with him, I don't want to discuss my health. Someday you'll understand what that's like." She patted Paris's hand. "Now, does London know?"

"I told him this morning before he flew to Florida."

"I bet it took some convincing to get him to leave." She shook her head. "I hope that son of mine won't be worried so much about me that he can't have a good time while he's there. He needs to enjoy the sun and beach for all of us stuck here in this freezing cold. It's supposed to snow tonight."

Paris couldn't suppress the laugh. Her mother always bitched about the snow and cold but when anyone suggested they move, she flat out refused. She might not like to be out in the snow, but her mother loved to watch it from the windows, to see the mountains with their white peaks.

"What's so funny?" Her mother raised an eyebrow at her.

"You…you know you love the snow as much as the rest of us." She shook her head before getting serious. "Mom, what am I going to do about Aiden and the other two men?"

"Go to Wyoming and see them."

"Aiden called to invite me there this weekend. He wants me to attend an informal barbeque with their parents so I can understand another aspect of their lives. But Mom, I can't. With London gone, I need to be here."

"When is this barbeque? London is due home on Friday but even if you're both gone things will be fine. Dottie is handling things for London while he's working away from the office. I'm sure she'll handle anything you need done here. Paul can pick up anything as well."

"It's Saturday, but this isn't a good time. I'm not just worried about work. You know I can manage that. I want to be here for you."

"Well, I'm putting my foot down. I want you to go. There's nothing more important in this world than finding the person or people you're supposed to spend the rest of your life with. I'll be fine and I'll be waiting to hear all about it. I want you to go and see if things can happen between you and these men. You've got to remember there's life outside the company."

"I agree," Paul said from the doorway.

"You were listening—" Amy started but Paul came up beside the bed and leaned down to kiss his wife, stopping her.

"Not the whole time, but I came back in from outside to tell you it was snowing and I heard the last bit." He stood by the bed, facing them. "Paris, you should have told me you felt drawn to them."

"Dad, you've told me from the beginning I need to be professional and not get attached to my clients. We both know London isn't the one to deal with Aiden and you need to be here with Mom. Why is this different?"

"You've never gotten bothered by clients no matter how attractive they are or what they say. It's different because your destiny is pulling you toward them. You're meant to be with them. You said it yourself, they're everything you've been looking for."

She looked from each of her parents before settling on her mother. "I want what you and Dads have."

"That's why you're going on Saturday because you deserve everything you want in life. Don't let those men slip through your fingers."

Her father laid his hand on her shoulder. "You'll go and claim your men just like your mother did with Mathew and me. Trust me, if those guys have a brain between them they'll be falling at your feet. Go call him and tell him you're coming. I'll make arrangements for Jake to fly you there. He can get a room in the area if things run late and you stay."

"Sweetie." Her mom squeezed her hand as she started to rise off the bed. "Go there as a woman, not as a matchmaker. A woman on a mission."

"Thanks, Mom and Dad. I love you guys." She leaned in and gave her mom a hug before standing to do the same with her father. When she stepped back, she eyed Dad. "You'll call me if anything changes, right?"

He glared at her, and her mother reached up and took Paul's hand. "Don't, hon. I know what Doctor Vander said and she didn't tell me."

"How?" He turned to Amy. "Why didn't you say anything?"

"I'll let you two sort this out and I'll get back to work. Dad, seriously, I want you to call me if anything changes." She didn't wait for an answer. London should be back as well, and she knew he'd tell her. Right now, her parents needed to work this out and she had work she needed to complete.

"Don't forget to call him," Mom called to her as she shut the door.

She wasn't going to call him right away, since she remembered he said he'd call her that evening. Making her way back through the house to her own quarters, her heart fluttered. Could she finally claim her destiny? After matching hundreds of people, was it her time to have the same happiness she created for others? *I hope so…*

What should have been a busy day of work passed with unnerving slowness until Aiden thought he was going to go crazy before it got late enough to call Paris. The time might have gone by quicker if the others had been around but Cody had work to do with the horses and Kain was dealing with one of the clients he represented, trying to nail down a contract. That left Aiden to his own business matters.

Throughout the day he'd found himself lost in thoughts about her, instead of actually getting any work done. Now that he could finally call her, he hesitated. What if she said no? What was their game plan if she turned them down? He wasn't sure, but the three of them would be back to square one when it came to courting her. *Maybe we'll make a trip to see her. I'm not letting her go without a fight, no matter how much she tries to avoid us.*

He plucked his cell phone from the desk and pulled up her number before bringing it to his ear. After three rings, his stomach sank as he started to think she wasn't going to answer.

"Hello." She sounded as if she were out of breath.

"Did I interrupt you in the middle of something?" He kept his tone steady and tried not to let his thoughts go in the direction they were. Was she seeing someone? Did they have competition? He wasn't sure how he'd feel if she had been busy with a gentleman friend.

"I just finished my evening run. I didn't hear my cell phone with my ear phones on."

Thinking of her hot and sweaty had his shaft hardening. "A woman who enjoys a good run, just my type." He pictured her plopping down on the sofa, cold water bottle in her hand, as she listened to him.

"Did you call for a reason, Mr. Dalton, or just to find out what my evening activities were?"

"You know why I called. Have you given more thought to my invitation?" Needing something to do with his hand, he rolled the pen on his desk.

"Actually…" She paused, sending his nerves spiraling out of control. "I'll come. Jake will fly me there Saturday morning, and will be on standby for when I'm ready to return. Is there anything I can bring?"

"Just your beautiful self." He gave her a moment to let his comment sink in before adding, "Cody's a pilot, he can come for you so Jake doesn't have to stand around waiting."

71

"Thank you, but you'll be busy with family."

"How about Cody takes you home then? There's really no reason to have Jake waiting around for you, when he can take you home whenever you're ready." He hoped she'd agree so they weren't on a time table to get her back to the airfield.

"Won't Cody be busy with his family as well?"

"No, only Kain and my parents will be here. Before you ask, you'll need to get the answer from Cody. That's his secret to share, not mine. Now, what do you say?" He'd tell her almost anything to get her here, but he wasn't willing to explain Cody's family. Even with the three of them being as close as they were, he had only found out the drama surrounding Cody's mother a few years before.

"Very well. You're right, it's crazy to have Jake waiting for me if Cody's a pilot. But…"

"But what?"

"If something comes up, and I might need to head out quickly, would Cody be willing to leave in the middle of things?"

"He'll leave whenever you're ready. We'll make sure the plane is gassed and ready to go in case there are any emergencies." He caught the fear that lingered in her voice. Even though she hadn't said as much, he was beginning to suspect the rumors of Amy Nelson's illness were true. He decided to approach it a different way to give her the opportunity to tell him. "Though I'm sure that the company will be fine for a day without you."

"No doubt, but things can come up."

She tip-toed around it, leaving him without a definite answer. He wouldn't pry; when she was ready, she'd tell them. "I'd suggest packing an overnight bag in case things go late. There's plenty of guest rooms, and you can stay here."

"I'm hoping to come home the same day. After all, you're not my only client."

"I have no doubt about that." He chuckled, thinking about how popular Beyond Monogamy's services must be now that their lifestyle was legal. "I look forward to seeing you on Saturday."

"Me too." For the first time since they began the call, there was a hint of excitement in her voice.

They spoke for a few more minutes before hanging up. Now that he had her answer, he felt like a weight had lifted off his shoulders. All he had to do was busy himself over the next few days before she arrived. Then they'd show her they were interested in her.

Paris Nelson, you're our destiny, and you're about to see that.

Chapter Eight

The week had gone by slower than a snail's pace. Everything seemed to take twice as long, the simple things Paris had once taken joy in suddenly seemed like a task. She had packed an overnight bag against her better judgment, along with files, and other work to keep her busy if she felt uncomfortable. Now that she was on the way to Wyoming her nerves were getting the best of her and she almost told Jake to turn the plane around.

She tried to calm her rolling stomach, but when she closed her eyes, images of her men filled her thoughts. Oh, how she wanted things to go smoothly this weekend. She'd never been this nervous before and she wasn't sure how to calm down.

"Miss Nelson, we've landed." Jake stood in the cockpit doorway. "Are you okay? It's so unlike you to pace the whole trip."

"I'm fine." How he knew she was pacing the jet was beyond her. Maybe he could feel the movements as he flew the plane. She'd hoped moving around and remembering her mother's reassuring words would relax her. She was making this journey to see if the four of them were as compatible as she thought, and if so she was there to claim her men. *My men.*

"I don't have anything planned if you'd like me to stay until you're ready. Even if you do end up staying the night, I don't mind."

She felt her stomach drop further as she remembered one of them was waiting for her just outside. "It's fine. Mr. Knight is a licensed pilot and can fly me home when I'm ready. There's no reason for you to wait here."

"Very well. Speaking of waiting, there's a black SUV and a gentleman outside." He unlocked and pushed open the door, lowering the steps for her. "Have a good time, Miss Nelson. You deserve this."

She grabbed her overnight and laptop bags and made her way up the aisle. "Thank you. Have a safe return trip." She stepped past him and headed down the step to the SUV that was waiting for her. Just as her heels hit the asphalt, Aiden came around the SUV and strolled toward her.

"It's good to see you again, Paris." He leaned down and kissed her cheek before taking her bags. "The others are back at the house setting up for this afternoon."

"I'm looking forward to meeting your family."

He placed the bags in the backseat before he opened the passenger door for her. "It's going to be a nice party, but the best part is that you'll be there."

Her heart skipped a beat at his comment as she wondered if there was a second meaning. She told herself she was just over-thinking things because of her own desires. Damn, she craved for him to want her as much as she wanted them.

Once inside the SUV Aiden nodded toward the plane at the end of the runway. "Cody came down this morning to get the plane ready for whenever you're ready. Though we'd like to have you stay the night, maybe we could have a peaceful brunch tomorrow and discuss things."

"We'll see how it goes." She didn't want to commit to anything but the idea of staying the night was appealing because it would give her more time with them. "The sky looks threatening."

"We're expecting a storm but it's not supposed to be that bad. Though it will be perfect for those who like to ski. Do you like to ski or snowboard?"

"It's been so long since I've been on the mountain, but I used to. Now it seems like all I do is watch it from the windows." She glanced at the mountains as he drove away from the landing strip. "What about you? Well, I guess not with your knee."

"Not anymore, I'm worried I'll blow my knee again. But Kain does."

"What about Cody?"

"Not much, he prefers sledging. He does carriage rides through the snow for people in town. Our Cody is a true romantic."

"Sounds like it." She nodded. The thought of taking a carriage ride through the snow with the men was truly enchanting; a romantic setting like that was sure to help her win their hearts. She debated briefly how she might go about getting Cody to take her and the others on one if she stayed.

She forced her thoughts away from the romantic notions and back to things that mattered. She needed to get to know them better, and not as prospective clients. "Kain and Cody told me about their work but you've been pretty quiet about it. What does your business entail?"

He looked at her for a moment before returning his gaze to the road. "It's not as exciting as working with horses, or having the clients Kain does."

"It's a part of you and that's what's important. You must enjoy doing it and keeping busy or you wouldn't still do it. Tell me about it."

"I'm an investor. I give loans to start-up businesses for a portion of their profit. If at the end of the loan period all investment and interest has been paid, they are free of any contractual obligations. If it hasn't, I come in and take over the business, sell, or we can extend the loan. If the business fails, they still have to pay the loan back, so I lose nothing. However, I'm selective on who and what business I'm willing to take a risk on."

"I don't know why you said it isn't interesting. Business has always been my thing and to me that's more interesting that any high profile client Kain has. Why haven't I heard your name tied to any company?"

He turned to head up the hill toward the house. "I prefer to remain a silent investor. I don't want someone's business doing well because I contributed to the funds to get it started or keep the business afloat."

"If you make money on a company doing well, then it seems like it's senseless to keep it quiet."

"True, but imagine someone going to a restaurant I've given funds to and the food not being up to par. It could affect all my other business transactions." He pulled the SUV to a stop in front of the house. "I need to keep my name as clean as possible if I want to continue occasionally doing sports casting."

"That makes sense." She nodded as movement from the front door caught her attention and Cody stepped out.

"Our parents will be arriving in a few hours but Cody wanted to talk to you while Kain and I finish getting things ready." He nodded toward Cody. "Go ahead and go with him, I'll take your bags inside and place them in the guest room."

Something about Cody caught her attention, and she realized she'd spotted a darkness she hadn't seen before. Deep within him, something was troubling him, but she couldn't put her finger on what it was.

As if sensing what she'd noticed, Aiden reached across the armrest and laid his hand on her arm. "He's got skeletons in his closet, but we all do. He's not a violent man, just closed off. Let him take his time telling you what he needs to."

"He doesn't have to tell me anything."

"Why, because you're just our matchmaker?" Something about his tone made her think he was searching, trying to figure out what was in her head. She wanted to be *more* to them, but she couldn't let on already.

"No, but there's no need to dig up the past."

"He thinks there is. Now go to him. I'll park in the garage and then take your things inside."

She opened her door and stepped down from the SUV. Cody reached for her arm, steadying her, and she turned to him. She wanted to wrap her arms around him and chase away the memories that were haunting him.

"I thought we could take a walk to the barn and I can show you the horses while they finish setting up."

"Sounds great. I've wanted to check out your horses since you mentioned them. Don't laugh, but I've never seen one in real life."

"A lot of people haven't." He tipped his head to a black four-by-four sitting on the edge of the driveway. "We could take that and be there quicker but it's just a short walk and it's beautiful."

"Let's walk and you can tell me about the horses." She figured that would help ease a bit of the tension within him.

Immediately his shoulders relaxed as he began to tell her about the different horses he owned. Describing each of them down to their breed, color, and even their personalities. It wasn't just how he chose to make a living, it was his passion. His face lit up as he talked about them.

"Did you know you can tell if a horse is cold by feeling behind their ears? If that area is cold, so is the horse."

"I guess I never thought about it. I just figured they'd have a way to keep themselves warm, but then again you see those horses with the blankets over their backs in the winter." She paused as they came to stand before the doors to the barn. "When I was a kid, I always wanted a pony. I never got one but it was my childhood wish."

"Why didn't you get one?"

"Mom said it was too much work since Beyond Monogamy was in the shadows then, and Mathew's law firm was touch-and-go because the town's residents suspected something happening between Mom and my two Dads."

"If you'd have gotten one as a child he'd still be around for many years to come. Ponies live longer than horses and can live well into their fifties." He pushed open the barn door. "I don't have any ponies now but we borrow one of the neighboring ranch's ponies in the summer when we have certain groups of children here. I'm sure I can arrange for you to go there and visit with it tomorrow before we fly out if you'd like."

"I think I might be too big for a pony now." She giggled, stepping toward a chestnut horse who had his head sticking out over the half door.

"That's General. He's an American Quarter Horse."

"He's gorgeous. Can I pet him?" He nodded, and she timidly reached forward.

"Go on, he won't bite. The General is used to rougher stuff than you'll dish out. He's my main stallion for the children. Calm and easy going. He'll take anything the kids through at him with style."

She noticed how soft his coat was as she ran her fingers over the side of his head. The horse leaned closer, sniffing her with interest. "What's he doing?"

"He likes you. Now scratch him behind the ears, it's his favorite spot. Wait, while I grab something."

"Don't leave me!" She tried to keep the panic from her voice but failed.

"You're fine." He stepped around her. "Give him this."

She quickly glanced down, not wanting to take her eyes off General for too long. "An apple? Now?"

"It's for him." He laughed at her confusion before he laid his head against hers, his body pressed against her back. "He'll eat it right out of your hand. Like this." He took her hand, placed the apple in it and guided her closer to his mouth.

"Wow." She whispered as the horse took a bite from the apple. Though she wasn't completely sure if she was more impressed with the feeling of him pressed against her or what General was doing. She wished she could focus more on Cody but with the horse eating from her hand she had to make sure he didn't mistake any of her fingers for food.

When the apple was gone, he reached farther around her to scratch the horse behind the ears. "Big boy, we'll be back later and go for a ride."

"Where to now?"

"There's still more to see." He led her down the row of horses toward where the hay was stored. "First I want to talk to you."

"We don't have to do this." She offered as much for him as for herself. Their time together had been special and she didn't want to ruin it by digging up the past.

He took a seat on a bale of hay. "Yeah we do. Aiden told me you asked why my family wouldn't be here today."

"It's none of my business." She tried to get him to see reason, to force away the storm clouds that were forming in his eyes. "Please, Cody, just show me the horses."

"My life was pretty normal until my father died but then it all changed. I don't just mean that I was suddenly the man of the house and was expected to deal with the ranch. I gave up everything to keep that damn place afloat."

She sat down next to him and laid her hand on his leg. "You don't have to do this."

"You need to know to truly understand why I'm the man I am." He stared down at the floor as he continued. "I worked from sunup to sundown to keep that place alive. Everything I did or thought was about the ranch. I turned down scholarships for college so I could stay and keep the family legacy alive. The winter after I graduated, it was right before Christmas when I found out."

"What?"

"All the money I had made in selling hay, produce, eggs, slaughtering our cattle, and everything else was gone. My mother didn't use it to pay back the loan or the other bills." He pushed off the hay and marched to one of the empty stalls. "See, my mother had a problem gambling years before I was born. My father kept her in check, not giving her more money than she needed, and cutting her off altogether when she went back to her old ways. I didn't have that same power and she took off with the money. While I was working the land she was spending the money on bets. Toward the end she was too drunk to even tell me what had happened. I ended up finding out from the police, who'd been sent to get us off the property."

"Oh, Cody." She came to stand behind him, her hand on his back. "I'm sorry. I know it's not any consolation, but it was just land. What matters is family."

"Family…I lost the last of my biological family that day as well." He turned to face her. "My mother knew they were coming, she knew all along what would happen when she didn't pay the loan note." He collapsed on the cool floor of the barn. "She killed herself while I was out in the field. I found her when I went to tell her the police were there and we had to leave. I was so pissed. I came in screaming at her, cursing her for everything that was happening."

She sank down on her knees next to him and wrapped her arm around him. "Oh, sweet Cody."

"The days leading up to it, we fought all the time. She died thinking I hated her and there's nothing I can do to change that." He let his head fall back against her shoulder until their gazes met. "I didn't hate her, I was just angry. She threw everything away. That ranch had been in my father's family for centuries and I had expected to take it over someday. Now it's gone."

"But look at the life you have. Look at what you've done, all you've created. You have this school for the children in the area. It might not be the ranch you once had but it's something you built. More importantly you're surrounded by those who love you."

"I'm missing one thing." He ran his hand over her cheek. "We're missing you."

She couldn't believe her ears. "Cody, you're upset."

"Upset…or maybe now I know what I want. I want you."

"Have you forgotten the three of you are supposed to find a woman

82

together? What do the others thing of this? Have you even told them?"

"I have, and damn…they're going to kill me for telling you. We don't need your matchmaking because we've already found the woman we want to spend the rest of our lives with." He let out a light chuckle. "I'm going about this all wrong."

She joined him in the laugh before nodding. "I won't say you've done it gracefully but I won't hold it against you."

She pressed her head to his. At least he was laughing instead of living in the past as he had moments before. She held him, never wanting the moment to end, while still wanting to take away the memories that had brought them to the ground of the barn. Even in the midst of everything else his pain was still in the forefront of her thoughts. She'd figure things out about the men later. That night after the get together with their parents she'd make sure they sat down and discussed what Cody had said. She needed to know if everyone felt the same way and then she'd be able to decide how she was going to approach things. Every fiber of her being hoped they'd all want her. Because she wanted them, too.

 Chapter Nine

The party was in full swing and everyone was having a good time. Paris stood near the doorway watching them. They were one big family, not divided into their own groups. Even Cody, the only one without any family there, fit into the mix without any problems. An outsider wouldn't be able to tell that Cody wasn't born into the family. Aiden's parents were sweet and seemed completely excited about their upcoming wedding. Actually, it was a renewal of their vows to them, while the public could believe whatever they wished.

Then there were Kain's parents and the way one of his two fathers always seemed glued to their wife's side. They were such a sweet trio that she couldn't take her eyes off them. There was a love that radiated from them, and she wanted that. She wanted her husbands to look at her the way Mrs. Fitzgerald's husbands looked at her.

"Having a good time?" Aiden came up next to her, placing his hand on the small of her back.

"Yeah. Thank you for inviting me. Seeing the three of you with your family…it's a special time. Your parents are great and so sweet." Her gaze traveled slowly over everyone before she tipped her head back to look at him. "It doesn't matter how you came together, you're a family. What makes it even more special is the fact that you've invited Cody into the fold."

"He told you what happened, and you didn't call Jake back to pick you up."

She turned to him, cutting him off. "Why would I? He did nothing wrong. You don't honestly blame him for what happened, do you?"

"Aren't you a firecracker?" He shot her a smirk before continuing. "No, I don't blame him because I know the whole story. The question is, did Cody tell you everything? Or just that he thinks he's the reason his mother killed herself."

"He told me she was gambling the money and they lost their ranch because of it. Is there something else?"

"She had a warrant out for her arrest for attempted armed robbery. She was desperate and tried to rob a liquor store two towns over, in order to save the land. Crazy idea that almost got her killed. The owner came out from the back with a gun and she took off." He wasn't looking at her any longer, his gaze on Cody. "I didn't know him then but Kain did. Kain's father was the sheriff here and he called us to see if there was anything we could do to help him. Kain flew home to collect Cody that night and he's been with us ever since."

"Help him how? You'd have been in your, what...second year as a football player?"

"I'd just finished my first season as a pro-football player. The first team running back got injured and I got thrown into it. It was a big year for me and the team."

She nodded. "I remember you took them all the way, winning the championship and everything. That's when your career really took off."

"Yeah, the whole off season I was rushed from one commitment to another that my agent set up. Cody was there as a bodyguard when things got rough, a friend when things were calm. We bonded during the trip but it wasn't until a few years ago he actually told me what happened. I knew what Kain told me but I didn't know how it affected him."

"He seems okay."

"For the most part he is, but he has a hard time opening up to people. He needs someone to share his romantic side with. It's going to take time for him to open up to any woman, for fear he'll let them down just as he believes he let down his mother." He rubbed his fingers lightly along the curve of her shoulder. "He needs you to take your time with him."

"Me?" She turned enough to raise an eyebrow at him.

"I know he told you what we want."

"What is it that you want?" She needed to hear him say it.

"We want you." He let out a light laugh before rubbing his hand down her arm. "We put this whole thing together to sweep you off your feet. It was Kain's idea to have you here with our families so you can see how much we care for them. We were going to get rid of them early and work on seducing you."

"What if I wanted to leave tonight?"

"We were hoping the weather would work in our favor to keep you here." He tipped his head toward the wall of windows, where the snow was falling heavily already. "Paris Nelson, you strolled into our lives and we will never be the same. You're the woman we want and need."

"How do you know?"

"My mother, Christine, used to tell me the story of how she met Dad. I remember her telling me over and over when she was dying. After the hundredth time I heard it I finally asked her why she kept telling me the same story, there had to be other things she wanted to tell me. She explained that she needed me to remember the story because she wouldn't be there when I found the woman I'd spend the rest of my life with and she wanted me to trust my gut. See, when she met Dad she just knew he was the one. I thought it was the pain medication that made her remember it differently than it happened, but when you strolled into my office I knew she was speaking the truth because I felt it to. I know it sounds like something that only happens in those chick-flick romantic movies but it's the truth."

"Maybe with you but not with Kain." They both glanced to Kain who seemed to know they were talking about him because he looked up at them and smiled.

"Maybe not when you stepped off the plane. He'll admit he was an ass but he doesn't like change and he took that out on you. Things don't have to happen the same way for everyone. With my Dad and Susan it didn't happen that way. He was attracted to her, but it was my mother who pushed. She knew the family needed something more, and Susan was right for them. I was young and don't remember that, but from what I hear she completed us, made us a true family. The point is, things changed when Kain spoke with you."

"You're all in agreement on this then?"

He nodded. "Now we just have to convince you. So I'm going to shove the family out the door and we're going to enjoy a quiet night here and you can get to know us more than just for your questionnaire."

Before she could argue, he had left her side, and signaled to Kain and Cody as he neared them. She was left standing there completely stunned. She had expected at least some challenge. For one of them to tell her that her woman's intuition was off. Instead, she found them ready to fight for her. She was one lucky woman, and planned to see if they were really up for the challenge.

The sun streamed through the dozens of windows while Paris nursed her second cup of coffee. She had never been a morning person, but today had been rougher after being up half the night talking with the three of them. Thankfully, none of the others seemed to be morning people either, as they were quieter than they had been since she arrived. Or maybe no one was looking forward to her leaving that afternoon. She wished she could have stayed, but Mom had treatment on Monday and Paris wanted to spend some time with her while she was well enough for company.

Kain leaned back in the kitchen chair, his cowboy hat sitting on the table next to his coffee, and cleared his throat. "The others and I were talking last night after you retired to your room. We would love to have you come back next weekend if you're not busy."

She polished off the last of her coffee before Cody refilled it. "I have plans for Sunday evening, but the rest of the weekend I'm available. Though Jake is off, he's going to visit his sister in Virginia. He's leaving Thursday and will return on Tuesday, but I could catch a—"

"Don't even say commercial airline." Cody slid the chair out beside her and sat. "I won't hear of it."

"I can't continue to put you out by having you fly back and forth."

"You do no such thing. Now I'll hear nothing more of it." Cody took a long drink from his coffee mug. "So it's settled. You'll come back this weekend."

"Cody, if you'll be available, I could come back Thursday afternoon. I mean...if none of you care."

"Look at her squirm." Aiden smirked over his steaming coffee. "You're welcome here anytime. I don't know what the others have planned for Friday, but I'll make damn sure I'm available for you, beautiful."

"Well, it seems like everyone has gotten you alone except me." Kain scooted his chair back and grabbed his cowboy hat. "Would you like to accompany me on a drive? I can show you around our area before Cody here has to fly you home."

"Sure. Just let me check in back home and I'm all yours." She grabbed her cell phone off the table and headed back to her bedroom for some privacy.

On her way out she heard Kain ask, "Has anyone been able to find out if it's true? Is Amy Nelson sick again?"

"I approached the subject with her but she didn't answer," Aiden replied before she was out of hearing range.

She knew she'd have to tell them, probably should have already, but she didn't want to see the sympathy in their eyes. More importantly, she didn't want their pity. Trying to push it from her thoughts, she pressed London's name, brought the phone to her ear, and continued to her room. She'd get an update on Mom's condition before she returned to face their questions.

"My dearest sister, to what do I owe this?" London answered.

"I called to see how Mom is. How was the treatment yesterday?"

"Rough, just like every treatment so far. She wants to have Sunday dinner like we always do so the dads are forcing her to take it easy today." The cluck of his boots hitting the corner of his desk as he reclined let her know he was in the office. "You want to tell me what's going on with you? You rarely deal with clients face to face, and now twice in less than a week you've gone to meet someone."

"I can't right now." She knew she was only putting off destiny but she wasn't going to tell London who she was visiting until she knew where things were going. She knew what a fan London was of Aiden's, and she really didn't want to be pestered about things until she was certain they'd work out. An announcement like that needed to be made in person, not over the phone. "How about we grab lunch on Monday and talk?"

"I thought you were going with Mom for her treatment on Monday."

"I am, but once we get home we can go out for a nice quiet lunch, just the two of us. We never do that anymore. We're both always busy. What do you say?" The two of them had always been close because of their rough childhood but recently they weren't making enough time to do the things they used to. It was always about the company and the work constantly surrounding them.

"Okay, let's do it. There's a new Italian place across town that I've heard good things about and I know how you love good Italian food."

"Great. Now back to the second reason I called. Do you think Dottie could cover any office calls for me on Friday?"

"Taking off early to visit this mysterious friend again?"

"Yes. I'm leaving Thursday afternoon, but I'll be home Sunday afternoon in time for our family dinner. So, what do you say, will you let me borrow her?"

"It's time you get your own Dottie if you're going to be out of the office so much but you know she'll cover for you even if I said no. She's sweet on you."

"On both of us." She chuckled. "Dottie's been with us so long she's like another member of the family. How she puts up with either of our crazy work schedules is beyond me. Thanks, London, I owe you."

"We'll call it even if you spill this secret at lunch. I've never seen you this tight-lipped about anything. At least not when it came to me, we've always shared everything."

"I know, little brother, and all will be revealed on Monday."

"Hold on." London said something to someone in the background before turning back to her. "Mathew said for me to hang up. He needs to call you. Safe trip home, sis. Love you."

She didn't have time to return the sentiment before he hung up. She barely had enough time to pull her cell away from her ear before it was ringing again. She glanced at the caller ID and wasn't the least bit surprised when *Dad Mathew* came across the screen.

"What's going on, Dad? London said Mom was okay. Have things changed?"

"My spouses have just informed me who you're with, and I want you home right now!"

"Dad, have you lost your mind?" She couldn't believe what she was hearing. Mathew had always been the most sensible of her two dads, and now he was having a fit. Why, because she was with Aiden Dalton?

"You don't understand what kind of danger you're in there. I can't believe Paul let you go without your guards. Mom's treatments must be getting to him.

As soon as you're on your way safely back home, I'm going to give him a piece of my mind. I was too upset and worried about you to do it before."

"Dad, Aiden's a former football player. He doesn't court more danger than I have hanging over my head. I don't understand what all this fuss is about. If you're upset with me not having my guards, fine, I'll bring them along next time. I have some things to finish before I come home."

"This isn't about Mr. Dalton," he snapped. "If you don't get Mr. Knight to bring you home now I'll send Jake for you."

She leaned against the corner of her bed. "Dad, tell me what this is about."

"One of Kain Fitzgerald's clients—"

"I thought he only did sports law?"

"He does. He defended a baseball player three years ago who was on trial for killing his mistress when he learned she was pregnant. He was convicted and he blamed Kain for his conviction."

"He's still behind bars though, right?"

"No, and that's why you need to come home. He was released Friday after new evidence came to light a few months ago, and now he's out for revenge."

"A few months ago?" She scooted along the mattress to lean against the headboard and pulled her legs against her chest.

"It took time for the system to work and for him to be released. He never killed the mistress. It was his wife who did. When the police arrested her she confessed, she still had the clothes she wore that night covered in blood."

"Fine, so he's out, why would that put me in any more danger than usual?"

"Because he's coming after Kain, the man he thinks sealed his fate and caused him to spend over three years in prison. I don't want to see you get hurt because of this, now please come home."

"Dad, I love you, and thank you for looking out for me. I can't leave right now. There are some things I need to take care of first, but I'll be home later today." When Dad started to interrupt her, she added, "I need to hear Kain's side of things before I'll even consider coming home. If these are the men I'm supposed to spend my life with, then we need to be straight with each other. I can't run off scared."

"Paris, you are too hard headed like your mother. Do you at least have your weapon?"

"I never leave home without it, especially when I don't take my guards. You and Dad taught me well, I can protect myself. Plus, I'll be with Aiden, Cody, and Kain until we leave. Don't worry." She reached to the end of the bed where her laptop bag was and grabbed her pistol. She hadn't planned to need it but if a situation arose it would do her no good in the bedroom.

"I always worry about my little girl. Text me when you leave and we'll have guards waiting for you when you touch down. I love you, sweetie."

"I will, and I love you too, Dad." She didn't bother to tell him that she wasn't his little girl any longer because she'd always be that to him. No matter how old she got it would remain the same.

She ended the call and slid her phone into the pocket of her jeans before undoing her belt to add her gun. With it firmly in place, she took a deep breath and headed back to the kitchen where the men waited. She'd find out the full story before she made any decisions.

The moment she stepped into the kitchen Aiden rose from the table from where the three men were chatting and came to her, wrapping his arm around her shoulder. "Everything okay? Something wrong at home?"

"Home?" She looked up at him and his words finally registered. "No...no, they're fine."

"Then what is it?" His furrowed brow showed his concern.

"I spoke with my father, Mathew, and he mentioned something." She leaned into Aiden's embrace. "Kain, is there something you need to tell me?"

"What do you mean?" He set his coffee aside and turned toward her, the question clear in his gaze.

"The baseball player you defended when he was on trial for murder."

"Kings? What about him? You're angry I defended that guy? I was only second chair and that was because he demanded it, his career was on trial as much as he was."

"I don't care you defended him. I care that he's out and after revenge....that you didn't mention it."

"Kain?" Aiden's voice held a touch of anger.

"He's out of prison? How?" Kain just stared at her as if he couldn't believe it.

"Dad said there was new evidence that came to light. It was his wife who killed the mistress, not him. Damn it, when the police arrested her, she confessed and everything."

"What about the other charges? He still should be doing time even if new evidence came to light." Kain ran a hand over his face, now ghostly pale.

"Maybe you should start at the beginning." She pressed closer to Aiden, needing to feel him against her.

He slid his hand down her waist, bumping into the butt of the gun. He leaned closer and lowered his voice just above a whisper. "We'd protect you."

"What?" Cody took his gaze off Kain and glanced toward them.

She lifted the side of her shirt to show the gun and holster. "Dad asked me if I had my weapon in case things went bad. Having it in my laptop bag won't help me or any of us."

"We don't carry them on us but there are weapons stashed around the house in case of emergencies," Aiden reassured her. "Living this far out of town we have to rely on the county police and depending on where they are the response time can be lengthy."

"You can't count on anyone but yourself," Cody chimed in. "Home defense is a must here. I'm not talking about crime, or the fact that Aiden's business deals can sometimes bring trouble, or that Kain's clients have the potential to bring even more problems. I'm also talking about wild animals."

"I hate that you're scared because of me." Kain frowned at her.

She wanted to go to him, to ease the worry from his face, but Aiden held tight to her.

"Kain, I think it's time for you to tell all of us what happened with that trial. Cody and I were in New York when it was going on, so we only know a little more than Paris."

"You already know he was accused of murdering his mistress. When we went to trial, it seemed like an easy case to win. The evidence was flimsy. They had his fingerprints and DNA from the scene but he admitted being there that night. He went to talk to her about the baby and what they were going to do. He even mentioned to her about leaving his wife to be with her and the child. One thing lead to another and they ended up in bed. It was a little after two when he said he left her townhouse and returned home. Only he never arrived home."

"Where was he?" Cody pressed.

"According to him, he went to their downtown condo. He said he needed time to think, to clear this head. The security guard didn't remember him coming in but he could have taken the elevator from the owners' garage, which is what he claimed. Anyway, the biggest fault to the case was Kings didn't have an alibi. If he'd have gone home his security would have recorded him coming in."

"Okay, so he was falsely convicted. Why does he want revenge on you?" She ran her hand over Aiden's as he held her tight against his chest.

"He wanted to take the stand, to tell the jury where he was and how he couldn't have killed her because he loved her. They were going to get married once he left his wife." Kain grabbed his coffee cup and just stared into it. "The other lawyer and I discussed it. We felt his credibility was shot because he was cheating on his wife. To get up on the stand and announce he was going to leave his wife for her would have made things worse. It would have also brought in other evidence that we worked hard to keep out. Including one domestic abuse charge his wife filed and then later dropped with the explanation that she made it up to get back at him. Whether he abused her or not, I don't know, but I know bringing it in would have cost us the case."

"You lost anyway." She didn't mean for it to be rude but she had to point out the obvious.

He nodded. "When we had to decide if he was going to take the stand we didn't think we'd lose. We thought it was in the bag."

"He's pissed because you wouldn't let him take the stand?" Cody raised an eyebrow.

"He could have gone against the advice of his lawyers but he chose to agree with us and we wrapped up the case. He's pissed at me because he needs someone to blame. One thing about Kings is he never took responsibility for anything his whole life." Kain stood from the table. "I'll tell you one thing, he won't harm you…any of you. I'll damn well see to that."

Chapter Ten

The next few weeks went by without any sign of Kings or any problems for that matter. It had become routine for Cody to arrive on Thursday to fetch her and she had spent every weekend with them. They had used the time in the plane to get to know each other better, and he was even teaching her how to fly. She was on the right track if she wanted to get her private pilot's license and he promised to help her with the rest of the requirements.

The only thing that hadn't happened over the last couple of weeks concerned London. She still hadn't found the right moment to tell him who she was spending all her time with. First their lunch was canceled by unexpected work on his end, and then she was busy with Mom or her own clients. She had even interviewed two possible assistants but neither of them were the perfect fit.

Instead of worrying about business or her brother, she moved away from the window and glanced back to where Aiden was wrapping up a business call. He tapped his lap and she went to him. She curled into his lap, wrapping her arms around his neck, careful not to jar his headset.

"Very well." Aiden wrapped his arms around her waist, keeping her tight against his body. "Yes, I'll have my lawyer draw up the contract and send it to you. It should be in your email by tomorrow, end of the business day." He paused as the person he was talking to said something. "Yes. I look forward to doing business with you."

He pulled the headset off and nuzzled her neck. "My beautiful…" He kissed his way down the curve of her neck to her collarbone. "So sweet."

She arched into his touches, wanting things to go further. Affection and sweet caresses was as far as things had gone, and she was growing impatient. She wanted each of them. Her body ached for their touch.

"Aiden…" Her voice cracked as he dragged his teeth over the fleshy part of her shoulder. "I want you."

"You have me. All of me." His words were muffled as he worked his way back up her shoulder and neck.

"I want you in a way a woman wants a man." Suddenly uneasy, she wasn't sure how to tell him she wanted sex with him. "I want you naked."

He stopped mid-kiss and pulled back to look at her. "My beautiful woman, I've wanted you every moment since you walked into my life."

"Then why—"

"Have I waited so long?" He ran his hand up her back. "You deserved to be courted like a woman of your stature. The fancy dinners, parties, and everything else we can give you. Sadly, with this crap with Kings, we've been unable to do all the things I've wanted to do with you. I kept hoping it would go away so we could take you out on the town and show you a good time."

"I don't need that. Actually, I'm not sure that's my style. I don't mind occasionally, but all my life I've been a little sheltered, ditching the media and everything like that, so I've come to enjoy the quietness life has to offer. I couldn't be happier here with you and the others."

"You deserve so much more." He leaned forward until their foreheads were touching. "If you promise not to hold it against me when I drag you along to functions in the future, I'll let you in on a secret."

"What's that?" She smirked.

"I prefer to be home instead of Mr. Social. I don't mind family and friend events, but the functions where I have to be there for other reasons is a whole different ball game. Trust me, these will come up, but now I have a beautiful woman for my arm."

"These events…they'll be business related or because of your career? How are you planning to handle that with our relationship?" She leaned back so she could get a better look at him. "With my family business and my position within the company, there's no way we'll be able to keep the relationship between the four of us quiet, even if you wanted to. Not to mention, I don't want to live a life of secrets, not with all my parents have gone through for our lifestyle."

"Wow, beautiful. I never had any intention to do any such thing. The media will get hold of this soon enough, actually I'm surprised they haven't already. When they do, we'll face it like we should."

"How's that?" She raised an eyebrow at him.

"Head on with a news conference. It will give us a chance to clear things up from the start and then the media won't be able to run wild with their stories. As you said, with your family being so public about it, plus Kain and my business dealings, we're in the public eye, so we can't hide this."

"What about Cody? Is he ready for that? How will he feel if the parents stop bringing their children to his riding school?"

"He'll deal with it. All of us know what we're risking, but it's what we want. I hope you're not worrying that if our businesses dries up from this that we'll be out on the street."

She shook her head. "You already told me you're fine financially and that wasn't even a concern. I don't give a shit about the money. Cody does it because he loves it. It gives him something to replace the land his mother gambled away. Will my Cody still be the same without it?"

"We'll be fine because we have each other. He realizes what bigots some people can be. A few years ago, he lost a few of his students because their parents heard the three of us were sleeping together. He dealt just fine just as he will if anything happens now. Don't worry about any of this."

"How can I not? It reminds me our time is limited before the media finds out. How we've gone this long I don't know."

"How about I take your mind off it?" Without waiting for an answer, he pressed his lips to hers. Slipping his tongue between her lips, he devoured her, tugging her shirt up as he went. Breaking the kiss, he pulled her pale blue sweater over her head.

"I thought you had work?"

"Don't think, just feel." He kissed along her jawline until he reached the sweet spot below her ear. Grazing his teeth over the area, he blew his cool breath against her flushed skin. "Work can wait, this can't. I've wanted to have my way with you since you first stepped into this office."

"Office sex…" She moaned in pleasure as he nibbled and kissed his way down to her breasts. "How often I've thought of this."

He slid his hand around her body, quickly finding the clasp of her bra and unhooking it. The material slid down her arms, revealing her perky breasts, making his shaft strain against his slacks and press against her thigh.

Claiming her nipple with his teeth, he gently tugged, making it hard before moving over to the next one. Without breaking contact he reached behind her, gathering the papers and slipping them into a drawer. "We should be doing this in the bedroom."

"I have no doubt there will be plenty of time for the bedroom later. Right now, I want you here. You look so in control and demanding behind your desk. I want this to be where we first make love. After all the hours we've spent in here together, it's a special place for both of us."

"Beautiful, your wish is my command. I still think you deserve better."

She leaned closer, pressing her naked chest against him. "I've always wanted to make love on a desk. It makes me feel like a naughty girl."

"Let's check this one off your list and then you can tell me all the other places where you've wanted to make love." He picked her up and placed her on the edge of the desk, slipping his fingers under the material of her black dress slacks to slide them down her thighs.

"It might be a long list." She teased, working her fingers down the line of his shirt buttons.

"There are three of us and we have the rest of our lives to make sure every one of your dreams come true." He lowered her pants enough to see she was naked under them. "Oh woman, you're going to be the death of me."

She watched as his already hardened shaft bobbed against the fabric of his slacks, demanding freedom. "I could lie and tell you I forgot my panties at home but I think you'd prefer the truth. I've been wanting the three of you for long enough, I didn't want anything to stand in the way when things got to this level." She let her heels fall to the floor just seconds before he got her pants low enough that he could let go and they'd fall away.

"You should have worn a dress then." He smirked as she pulled the dress shirt off him and tossed it onto the chair behind him.

"Off with these pants. I want you as naked as I am."

He unzipped his slacks, letting them fall down his legs before kicking out of them and his dress shoes. "Is that better, beautiful?" He didn't give her a chance to answer. He crushed his mouth to hers, and slid his hand between her legs. Unerringly finding her core, he thrust his fingers into her as she moaned around his unrelenting kiss. He held her captive against his body, teasing her clit with his thumb. Fierce desire rose within her.

"Aiden, I want you," she murmured against his mouth, holding onto him as wild delight rushed through her.

His teeth grazed her lower lip and he pulled his hand away. She cried out in frustration, her climax halted, but he ignored her demands.

Without waiting he adjusted his angle, gliding his shaft over her opening, pulling a moan from her. Slowly he glided the length of him in, just a little at first, her nails digging into his back as he worked his way inside her tight passage. Halfway in he stopped and slid out, even as she clung to him trying to force him to stay.

Once he was out, he gripped her hips and slammed his length into her, filling her completely. He didn't give her time to catch her breath as he began rocking their bodies back and forth, each thrust gaining momentum.

He left her mouth and kissed a path to her neck. She was torn between leaning back to grab the edge of the desk so he could claim her nipples again with his mouth, or pressing herself tighter against him with each thrust.

She didn't have to decide, he decided for her. "Lean back. I want to watch your breasts bounce as I take you."

She leaned back, grabbing the edge of the desk, her body arched toward him. With every thrust her breasts bounced with appreciation, calling to him. Without losing his rhythm, he dipped his head and drew his tongue along each nipple, blowing gently on them.

"Aiden," she cried out, her release within reach.

With one last tug on her nipple he let it slide free from his mouth, then placed his hands on her hips again, gaining more control as his pace sped and her climax began to peak. Tension had her muscles constricting around him as her orgasm neared. She leaned into him, digging her nails into his shoulders she held on to him, every pump of his hips sending pulses of pleasure exploding through her. She came apart at the seams, her inner muscles clenching to him as he continued to drive into her.

Her moans echoed off the walls as her world exploded, and his name tore from her lips. He pushed into her again before his own ecstasy had him exploding within her. His moans mixed with hers.

"Wow." Her voice was low as she tried to regain her breath.

He laid his head in the crook of her shoulder. "I love you, Paris."

She had waited so long to hear those three little words because she had known for the last several weeks that she had fallen in love with them. She wrapped her arms around his neck. "I love you."

A knock on the door interrupted him before she could suggest a second round. "Damn, just when I thought I had you all to myself."

"One moment," he called out. Then he slipped out of her, grabbed his slacks from the floor and pulled them back into place.

"I'll just slip into the bathroom and get dressed." She smirked before she gathered her clothes and took her escape.

As she closed the bathroom door she heard him say, "Come in."

She leaned against the bathroom counter, her face flushed, and her body relaxed. She quickly slipped into her clothes while Kain's deep voice drifted through the door. She ran her fingers through her hair, trying to fix it, before she felt presentable enough to open the door.

She found Aiden, his dress shirt still open with Kain reclining in one of the chairs across from the desk, a knowing grin on his face. Sometime throughout the day his cowboy hat had been tossed aside leaving his hair slightly flattened to his head.

"Well, darling…" Kain called to her and patted his lap. "Here I thought I'd be the first one to take you to bed."

She sauntered toward him. "Why's that?"

He pulled her down into his lap, leaving her legs hanging over the side of the chair. "Well, when you arrived you thought Aiden was a ladies' man and I figured Cody would be too shy to advance without you leading the way. So, I thought it would be me."

"I don't think of him as a ladies' man, and Cody's not shy with me any longer." She rested her head against his chest. "Don't worry, you'll get your chance."

"Now?"

"Eager, my sweet cowboy?" She rubbed her hand up his chest, wishing she could slip it under the polo pullover he wore.

Aiden stood before them, buttoning his shirt. "I hate to damper this but there's someone waiting for a legal contract from you. Have you had time to look over the file yet?"

"I have and that's what I tossed onto your desk when I came in. Now, darling, how about we leave Aiden to work."

"What did you have in mind?" She stood but kept her hand in his.

"Come upstairs and we'll see what trouble we can get into."

The way he said upstairs she knew it could only mean one thing, the room with the view at the top of the house. The sun would be sitting soon and that very idea had her recharged enough to want him in the same way she had Aiden. "Come on, cowboy, it's time to show me what you're made of."

Chapter Eleven

Jazz music from the record player echoed through the room while Paris stood by the window, watching the sun sink low in the sky. A few weeks ago Kain had revealed his passion for jazz music played the old fashioned way. Until meeting him, she had never been able to appreciate jazz; she wasn't sure if it was his taste in music or that it had grown on her because she loved him. Either way, it had set the mood.

He came up behind her, wrapped his arms around her waist, and nestled his head into the crook of her shoulder. "You're beautiful in this light."

"I think it's the sunset that does it."

"No darling, it's you. I only have eyes for you." He kissed her neck. "Dance with me."

"I left my dancing shoes downstairs." She looked down at her bare feet.

"That's good for my toes. I'm not the best dancer in the world. If you want a good dance partner you need Aiden or even Cody. But you standing here with the sun cascading around you, I want to have you in my arms."

"Dancing isn't everything. I prefer a man who can cuddle over dancing any day."

He pulled her into his arms, keeping his hands at the small of her back. "I'll cuddle with you anytime you want. I'll show just how well I cuddle here shortly."

"Promises, promises."

"Tonight there are no promises. I'm going to show you what kind of man you've hooked." He began to sway to the beat of the music before leading her around the room in a slow dance. "I knew you'd be a great dancer."

"Kiss me."

"I like a woman who knows what she wants." He leaned his head closer to her. His warm breath hit her cheek a moment before his lips claimed hers.

She wrapped her arms tighter around his neck, drawing him closer to her. He was the shortest of her men but there was still a good five inches that separated her from his six-foot-two frame. Their tongues mingled together to match the desire coursing through her. She wanted him with every ounce of her being.

He took her hand in his and led her toward the sofa. "We need to put a bed up here for times like this but tonight the sofa will work. I want to see the last rays of sun reflect off your gorgeous naked body."

"I don't care where we are. I just want you." She grabbed hold of his cowboy hat and slipped it on top of her head before working her way to the buttons of his jeans.

"Woman, you look better in my hat than I do."

She managed to get his jeans undone enough that she could slip her hand between the rough material. She freed his shaft from the constraints of his boxers, running her hand down the length of his hard-on. "I thought it was required in Wyoming that when you were going to break a cowboy you must wear the cowboy hat. Too bad I don't have the boots to go with it."

"Break me? Hmmm. My little woman is cocky."

"I'm going to break you from thinking of any other woman, ever again." Her hand tightened along his shaft, drawing a moan from him.

"I've always been a one woman man, darling. You don't have anything to worry about. Now off with these clothes before we lose the rest of the light and I have to tear them from you."

Neither of them wasted time stripping and came together on the sofa. She slid her hand along his chest, feeling his smooth skin and tight muscles. Then she dropped to her knees before him, sliding her hand down his chest until she could take hold of his manhood. Gently she caressed her hand down the length of him.

"Darling." He tried to pull her back up to him.

"Let me." She leaned forward, kissing the tip of him before letting him slip between her lips. Taking him into her mouth, her hand worked at the base, and he tangled his hand in the strands of her hair, holding her close. Her mouth worked up and down the length of him, milking the life out of him.

He moaned her name before placing a hand on her shoulder. "Not like this, I want to be inside you and tonight I won't last long."

She let him slip from her mouth and he pulled her up, lifting her to the sofa. He kissed her neck, nibbling down her jawline to her shoulder. She let him have a few more minutes of exploration, since he'd finally made it to her breasts. He wrapped his mouth around her nipple, flicking his tongue over the bud, drawing it to full hardness. He teased over the other one, tweaking it until it stood at attention. Her nipples had always been extra sensitive, the slightest touch bringing her pleasure. She moaned in ecstasy when his tongue flicked over one hardened tip.

"Kain." Her voice betrayed the desire that rushed through her.

He let her nipple slip from between his lips as he gazed up at her. "Yes, darling?" His eyes gleamed and his lips curved up into the cocky smile she had come to know was all him. He grabbed her hips and pulled her so she was straddling him. "You wanted to be a cowgirl; I'm going to give you a chance to ride me."

He caressed every inch of her body, sending moans of ecstasy from her lips. His touch was incredibly tender, as though trying to memorize every curve of her body with his hands and mouth. Heat soared through her blood, like a fire burning just below the skin, impatient and demanding. He kissed a path down her neck, his thumb playing over her nipple. Sensations collided and threatened to overwhelm her when he teased her nipples. She wiggled her hips, his shaft rubbing against her folds. "Please, Kain, I want you."

With every touch, she arched her hips, demanding more. She couldn't get enough of him. Nudging her legs farther apart, he delved inside her and she met the teasing thrusts. A demanding moan she barely recognized vibrated in her throat.

"Kain…" She cried out, needing him more with every touch.

"Darling, you ready for the ride of your life?" He spread her legs farther, giving him the access he needed before filling her slowly, inch by inch. Halfway in, he slid out before thrusting back in, filling her completely with his manhood. His strokes fed her fire like tinder set to dynamite, until the heat between them blazed.

He increased pace, driving the force of each pump. The erotic dance amped up her tension; every delicious glide of his shaft inside her seemed to set off another cascade of heat. Their bodies rocked back and forth, tension stretching her tighter as she fought for the release she longed for.

"Kain." She clenched her muscles tightly around him.

He pressed his lips over hers, claiming her cries with his mouth. Their breath became ragged as he rocked in and out, finding the perfect rhythm, bringing ecstasy within reach. Upon that release, she dug her nails into his back, arching her body into his, her head thrown back in pure ecstasy. He continued to drive his shaft into her, until with one final slam home his own release followed.

"My gorgeous cowgirl." He held her against his body, his shaft still nestled deep within her as their breath began to return to normal.

The sun had sank below the horizon long before they were ready to move. Paris snuggled next to Kain, her head resting on his shoulder, just being together. They didn't need to talk. It was a comfortable silence, cuddling after the bliss of amazing sex. Her body was a little sore from the activities over the last few hours but she wouldn't have changed a thing about it.

Two down, one last man to claim. Even with her thoughts drifting to Cody, she had no desire to end this time with Kain.

"Get dressed, we need to talk." Aiden's rich voice came through the doorway, but as she glanced toward it she didn't see him.

"Hey, man, I gave you your time with her. We'll be down in a bit." Kain held tight to her.

"It's important or I wouldn't interrupt. Now dress."

Reluctantly Kain let her slip from his arms. She quickly slipped her dress slacks back on and her bra, while Kain slid into his jeans. Still partially undressed she called to Aiden, knowing that whatever he had interrupted them for must be important. "Get in here and tell us what's going on." She pulled her sweater over her head, now fully dressed. Kain was busy putting his cowboy boots on, his chest still bare.

"You left your phone on my desk and when Paul couldn't get through to you on it, he called mine." Aiden closed the distance to her just as her knees began to shake.

"Mom..." She'd have collapsed onto the floor in a heap if Aiden hadn't wrapped an arm around her, keeping her upright and pressed to his chest.

"Shhh, beautiful. It's going to be okay." He rubbed small circles up her back. "Cody wanted to be here but I sent him on ahead to get the plane ready."

"Is she...dead?" Her voice broke as images of her not being there during her mother's last moments filled her thoughts.

"Mathew went to wake her for dinner and found her unresponsive. She's been admitted to the hospital, critical care. She's in a coma."

"Momma." Tears rolled down her face and she held onto Aiden. Kain came up behind her, wrapping his arms around her and cuddling against her back.

"Why didn't you tell us she was sick?" Still holding her tight, Aiden kissed the top of her head.

"It never seemed like the right time. Coming here was my escape. I love my family, but since Mom got sick, London and I have had to take over the company completely. I'd never admit it to them but it's been stressful. Since the new laws have passed, the company has grown beyond expectations. Dad wanted me to hire an assistant but I'm a control freak." She knew she was rambling but talking about the company helped to calm her. "I just didn't want to drag you into it."

"You asked if she had passed. Was there a time frame given?" Kain ran his hand up along her arm.

"Unofficially yes." Her voice broke and she laid her head against Aiden's chest. "If the chemotherapy and radiation combination doesn't work she won't make it to the first thaw."

"Darling, you should have told us. It's too hard to keep something like that bottled up inside you." Kain squeezed her a little tighter to him.

"I've got to go to her."

"I know." Aiden nodded. "Cody's gassing up the plane now."

"I'll gather things for all of us." Kain kissed her cheek before stepping away from her.

"What?" She turned her head enough to look at him but he was already walking out the door.

"We're going with you." Aiden pressed his finger to her lips. "Don't tell us we don't need to. We're coming. You need us."

"You all have your own things going on. Your business transaction from earlier, Cody's horses."

"It will be fine, beautiful. We'll get the neighboring ranch to send one of his hands over to care for the horses while we're gone. He's always willing when we need to travel. As for the business deal, it isn't as important as you are, but it too will be fine. Kain and I can do whatever work we need to remotely. He'll grab our laptops, along with the rest of the things we need. Kain's resourceful when it comes to things like this, and I can care for you."

"I haven't told London…"

"About your mother?" He raised an eyebrow at her.

"No, about you." Her mind was racing, and she wasn't sure why she was worrying about something that was so inconsequential compared to her mother's illness.

"I'm still confused, beautiful. He doesn't know you've been coming to see someone?"

"He knows I've found someone…romantically…but he doesn't know it's you. You as in Aiden Dalton, former pro-football star." She ran her hand alone his cheek. "My baby brother is a big fan of yours."

"Ahh, I see now, but that was years ago."

"Not for London." She smiled, thinking about the picture that hung right next to her brother's desk. "There's a signed photo of you next to his desk…it's from when you played in college. He was a fan before you made it big, and not playing any longer hasn't changed that."

"How did he get that?" Aiden's brow furrowed. "I only signed one for Professor O'Clare."

"He's Dottie O'Clare's brother, and Dottie is London's personal assistant. Before she started working for London, she worked with my father Paul. They were there with London visiting a client who lived in the area and stopped by to visit her brother. London didn't want to sit around, so he made his way down to the football field where you were playing. It's been history ever since."

"Damn." He shook his head. "Doesn't matter, I'm sure he has other things on his mind right now."

"We might get off the hook for a bit but it won't be long." She snuggled against his chest, enjoying the feeling of his arms around her. "You know that's why I took your case. I don't normally do a lot of face to face stuff with clients, I'm more the matchmaker behind the scenes. Dad needed someone to cover for him and he came to me, because he knew how London would react to who it was. We didn't even put your information in our system and *every* client past or present is in the system."

"Well, I for one am glad you came to us."

"Me too." She smiled and lean to kiss him. It was chaste compared to earlier but it was all she could manage. "Mom knew all about you and after my first visit she told me to get my butt back here and claim my men. Little did I know when I arrived for that family celebration that the three of you had your own plans in mind."

"In the end we all got what we wanted." He pulled her back against his chest, holding her tight. "We'll be right by your side and we'll make sure you get through this."

"I've brought the SUV around to the front. We need to get a move on it, the snow is starting," Kain called from the bottom of the steps.

"We're coming." He let his hands slide down her back. "You ready, beautiful?"

"I just wish I was there already."

"We'll be there soon, Cody's waiting for us with the jet ready." He kept his arm around her waist as they made it down to Kain.

"I've got to grab my bags."

"I've already got them in the SUV." Kain held out her coat for her to slip her arms into.

Aiden put his own coat on before touching her arm. "Don't look like that."

"Like what?" She let Kain button her coat because her fingers just wouldn't stop shaking for her to do it herself.

"You're looking around this place like you'll never see it again. We'll be back."

"Oh, Aiden…Kain." Tears rolled down her cheeks again. "If this is prolonged I might not be able to come back for a while. My family will need me."

"Then we'll stay with you." Kain wrapped his arm around her shoulders. "We're a team, all of us, and we'll make this work."

Even as her heart broke and her hands trembled, she couldn't help but feel blessed because of the men in her life. They were truly the best the world had to offer and they were hers. She loved them even if she hadn't said the words aloud to all of them *yet*.

Chapter Twelve

The hour was late and the hospital was deserted by the time they had arrived. Paris walked hand in hand with Aiden and Cody, leading the way through the emergency room and heading toward the critical care wing when security stepped into the hall blocking the way.

"The hospital visiting hours are over. Unless your family was taken from the emergency room, you'll have to wait until morning." The taller security guard crossed his arms over his chest.

Anger rushed through her. It was unreasonable, but she couldn't help it. She had made it all this way and she wanted to get to her family. To find out what was going on and possibly see her mother. Her family needed her and she needed them. No security guard was going to stand in her way.

Kain laid a hand on her shoulder, giving it a gentle rub. "Darling, I've got this." He stepped around them and closer to the security guards. She wasn't sure what he said but whatever it was, they nodded and stepped aside. "Come on, darling."

She let go of Aiden and Cody's hands to wrap her arms around Kain's neck. "Thank you."

"It was nothing. They were only doing their job, once I explained the situation it was fine. Now let's get to your family." He kept his arm around her waist as they carried on down the hall, the others just a step behind them.

They made it down the rest of the hallway toward the first floor critical care unit without any problems. She glanced to the closed doors and she knew somewhere behind those pale blue doors her mother lay in a coma. She wanted to go there, to demand the staff let her in to see her mother, but that would do no good. What she needed to do was find her family, who were in the waiting room.

"Paris." Paul stood in the doorway to the waiting room looking completely worn out.

"Dad!" She slipped from Kain's arms and dashed toward him. "Oh, Dad, how is she?"

He pulled her into his arms, burying his head in her hair. He just stood there and hugged her. She hugged him back because she knew he needed it, while her men stood behind her giving them the space they needed. When he finally stepped back, he nodded for them to come into the waiting room. He led them toward the only round table in the room where they could sit together. Paul sat beside her, while Aiden took her other side and the other two took the last seats.

"Mathew's with Mom, but there's no change. Doctor Vander believes this reaction might have been caused by her newest medication but he's running tests to be sure. Right now we just have to wait. There's no telling when she might come out of it or if she will. The staff have been nice enough to understand our situation and have allowed one of us to stay with her at all times. There's also a private security guard at her door round the clock."

She glanced back at London who was spread out over one of the sofas, looking extremely uncomfortable. "He should have gone home to rest."

"He refused to leave." Paul glanced to the men before his gaze settled on Aiden for a moment. "You're going to have a hard time explaining why you've kept this quiet."

She reached beside her and took Aiden's hand in hers. "I've already told him all about London being a fan. Still, he was willing to risk family drama to be by my side."

"Thank you all for bringing my daughter home." Paul looked from each of them before back at her. "I'm sorry to have to call you home like this."

"Don't, Dad, you had no control over this and this is where I want to be."

"There were guards who were supposed to meet you at the airport. Didn't you see them?" Paul looked at the doorway as if expecting them.

"I sent them away."

"You did what?" He raised his voice, his eyes widening.

"Dad, I have these three with me. I didn't need any more of an entourage and this is a family matter. We didn't need this place crowded with guards while we're dealing with Mom's health." She laid her hand over his, trying to calm him.

"We'd have kept Paris safe," Cody added.

"He's right." Aiden nodded in agreement.

"Dad…" She squeezed his hand, drawing his attention back to her. "You said the medication might have caused this. Is there something they can give Mom to reverse the side effect?"

"They've taken her off the medication and now we just have to wait. It could take seventy-two hours for the drugs to completely leave her system. Paris, there's just nothing we can do but wait. Doctor Vander has consulted with some of the best doctors in the world and we just have to wait. I'm sorry."

"Then why don't you get some rest? You'll be no good to Mom if you're exhausted. I'll be right here and if anything changes I'll wake you." She nodded to the sofa he must have been using sometime before they'd arrived; there was already a pillow and blanket on it.

"Sir, your daughter is in safe hands," Aiden told Paul when he hesitated.

"I have no doubts there. My baby girl wouldn't have chosen just any men.

She'd want ones who would make her feel safe." He laid his hand on her shoulder. "That's the very least you deserve after the danger we've put you in."

"Dad—"

"I know, I know. Don't give me that speech again." He rose from the table. "I'm going back to check on Mathew and Mom. When I come back with an update, you can go home and get some rest. There's nothing you can do here tonight and you know I'll call if she wakes up."

"I just got here, there's no way I'm leaving." She glanced at her men, feeling slightly guilty because she knew they wouldn't leave without her, but she hadn't flown all this way to go wait at home.

"You're as stubborn as Mom, so I know you'll do as you want. I don't have the strength to argue with you. Why do you think London is still here? I gave up fighting him to go home and rest. How did I manage to get saddled with two stubborn kids?" Paul mumbled as he made his way from the waiting room to the critical care unit across the hall.

"He's right, you need rest." Cody moved from where he had been sitting to the chair next to her.

"I'm not going anywhere."

"Then lay down on the sofa. We'll wake you if anything changes," Aiden suggested.

She brushed off their touches and rose from the table. "I'm not tired." She stalked over to the small kitchenette. She needed something to keep her hands busy, to keep her from bashing someone with her anger. Losing it now would bring nothing but tears. Still, that wasn't what kept her together; it was the fact that her family needed her. Dad could walk back through that doorway at any moment and he didn't need to see her falling to pieces.

Hadn't their family had to deal with enough already? Cancer had been eating away at Mom and the family for long enough. They needed a break…they needed the treatment to work.

"Hon…" Aiden whispered, his arm around her shoulder as his other hand came around to lay over hers on the coffee pot. "Give me this."

She didn't understand what he wanted until she realized she had made a mess. Coffee flowed over the mug, spilling over the counter and dripped onto the floor. "Shit!" She let him take the pot and grabbed napkins to clean up the mess.

"Cody." In a flash Cody was by their side, taking the napkins from her and Aiden pulled her away. "Come on, hon. Cody will clean it up and bring you a fresh cup. Just come sit with me." He didn't wait for an answer and next thing she knew, she was being pulled down onto his lap.

Kain wrapped a blanket around her shoulders. "Darling, we can handle things. Just stay here with Aiden and Cody, I've got to step into the hall and make a call." He kissed her forehead before he walked away from them.

"Wonder if they've eaten…maybe I should get Dad something from the vending machine…"

"Stop worrying about everyone else." Aiden rubbed his hand along her back. "You're stressing yourself out more."

"Here." Cody sat on the edge of the sofa, next to her legs that were hanging over the side of Aiden's thighs. "Drink this. The warm liquid will help you and I'll deal with making sure your parents have eaten."

She took the mug from Cody; thankfully he had considered her shaky hands and had only filled it halfway. No doubt Aiden was thankful for that as well, since he wouldn't get hot coffee spilled over him. "I've got to do something."

"What you need to do is let us care of you. I'll make sure your family eats, drinks, sleeps, and anything else you want, as long as you let us do the same for you." Cody laid his hand on her thigh. "There's nothing you can do right now but wait. Let us comfort you."

"Come on, beautiful, rest." Aiden continued to rub small circles along her back. "You know we'll wake you up if anything happens."

"Just hold me for a minute and then I will." She let Cody take the untouched coffee and laid her head against Aiden's chest.

"I'll hold you for as long as you want." He placed a soft kiss on her temple.

Cody lifted her legs and sat next to Aiden, her legs over his, gently massaging her calves. It was comfortable and her eyelids were growing heavy; she only wished Kain was there with them. She felt like a piece of her was missing with him gone. She placed her hand on Aiden's chest, and realized the four of them had become a team. She might have been the final piece that had brought them together but they were the ones who made her realize there was more to life than work. Love was more important than work and money. *The love of these three men is worth more than anything in this world.*

Paris wasn't sure how long she had been asleep in Aiden's arms but she came awake to hear London's voice. Exhaustion hung heavily on her, so instead of rolling over to see what was going on she snuggled against Aiden's chest and did her best to block out everything around her.

"Could you keep your voice down and let her sleep?" Cody asked, nicer than the other two would have.

"But you're Aiden Dalton. What are you doing here? More importantly why are your hands on my sister?"

"I'm here with her." Aiden gently rubbed her back. The touches held a hesitation that wasn't there before, as if he was torn between wanting her awake and wanting her to rest.

"She doesn't need a man who will toss her to the side whenever he's tired of her. You've left a line of women behind you and she will *not* be one of them."

Aiden chuckled, his chest vibrating her head. "Your sister said you were a fan…I hadn't expected this reaction."

"Fan or not, I won't stand by and let you hurt her."

"The days you're talking about are long gone and you don't know the full story." He laid his other hand on her arm. "I'm not going to hurt Paris, I love her."

"Damn it, London, this isn't the time," Mathew growled. "Let your sister sleep and leave the guys alone."

"Dad, it's okay, I'm awake." She reached up to cup Aiden's cheek. "My sweet man, I love you." She didn't care that her family was watching, she ignored them and leaned up until she could kiss him. Her tongue slid between his lips. She kept it sweet, even as the desire to straddle him and devour him coursed through her. With one last peck she forced herself to lean back; even as she did so, she could see the desire in his eyes.

"If I knew that was all it took to get a kiss like that..." Kain shook his head.

"Paris..." London started only to have Mathew grumble at him. "Dad, I'm just looking out for her."

She slipped off Aiden's lap and rose to stand in front of her brother. "First, you heard Dad say now isn't the time. Second, I love you little brother, but I know what I'm doing. The media trashed us in ways that were unbelievable and they did the same to Aiden. He's always been upfront to me about his past. Now please just drop this."

London held his hands in front of him. "I'll let it go *for now*."

Instead of fighting the inevitable, she stretched and looked at Dad. "Any change?"

"No." He set aside his coffee. "Paul's with her and the new doctor."

"New doctor? Dad didn't say anything about another doctor."

"Kain..." Mathew nodded to Kain who was sitting on the arm of the sofa.

"Doctor Tobias he's a neurologist who treated Aiden after a rather nasty hit when he was playing ball. We've kept in touch over the years and he's one

121

of the best in his field. I called him in to give your family a second opinion."

Kain's explanation brought a fresh wave of tears to her eyes. "Oh, Kain!" She went to him, only to have him draw her tight against his chest.

"It was nothing, darling."

"It means everything to me." She tipped her head back so as not to get tears and makeup all over his shirt.

"Excuse me." A man stepped into the doorway. "Are you all Mrs. Nelson's family?"

"Doctor Tobias, please come in." Kain held out a hand to him, without taking his other arm from around her waist. "It's good to see you again, though I wish it was under better circumstances."

"I'm afraid this is how I normally run into people." The doctor took Kain's hand and shook it. "If you could help me gather Mrs. Nelson's family. Mr. Nelson will be joining in a moment and I'd like to tell them their options."

"We're all family." Mathew rose from where he had been sitting. "I'm afraid the coffee isn't very good, but can I get you a cup?"

"I'm fine. Thank you." Doctor Tobias glanced around the room. "Everyone might be more comfortable if we sat."

"Please, Doctor Tobias…tell us how my mother is." Her chest tightened and black spots danced along her vision. She blinked trying to get them to disappear.

"Yes, what did you find when examining my wife?" Paul asked as he closed the door to the waiting room, giving them privacy.

Paul went to stand next to Mathew and suddenly she saw something she hadn't seen between her dads before. There was a bond like what her men had. They shared a love similar to what they shared with Mom.

Doctor Tobias looked around the room before his gaze settled on Paul and Mathew. "There's no medical reason your wife should be in this coma. They had already started the process to clean out her system before I arrived.

However, from my research on the drugs she was on there was no alarm that was set off that should have caused this. It could be how her body is reacting to the drugs, chemotherapy, and radiation."

Needing to be a part of the conversation instead off to the side, she took Kain's hand and walked across the room to stand next to Paul. "Is there anything we can do?"

Paul wrapped his arm around her shoulder. "Is there? Because so far you've given us the same information we've already heard from the other doctors."

"This is where my colleagues and I differ." He glanced to Kain before looking back at Paul. "Kain brought me in because of an experimental drug that I've helped develop. It's still in the testing stage and hasn't been approved yet. I think it might be helpful to your wife."

"Hold on." Mathew's body stilled. "What kind of risks are we talking about?"

"Mom shouldn't be experimented on like she's a lab rat." London shook his head.

"If there's a chance to save Mom, don't you think we owe her that? Would you want to be in a coma as life rushed by you?" She squeezed Kain's hand, hoping he knew what he was doing by bringing Doctor Tobias in.

"Mathew's right, we need to know the risks before we could even consider this." Paul rubbed her shoulder.

"I've studied cancer patients who have lapsed into comas for what seemed like no reason at all. Could have been the strain of the cancer, the treatments, or the medications. Medicine has come a long way in the last fifty years and we're still learning how all these changes affect our bodies. This drug has been beneficial in helping to bring over seventy percent of the patients out of their comas."

"What happens to the other thirty percent?" She felt her stomach sink as possibilities ran through her thoughts.

"Most remain in the coma, possibly never regain consciousness." Doctor Tobias paused. "Less than five percent have died, either because of the drug or because their bodies have just been through too much and they couldn't handle anything more."

"We can't risk Mom. Dads, you've got to see that. Look at our luck lately."

"London, I understand your concern but we can't leave her like she is." Mathew looked to Paul and then Paris. "What do you think?"

"Mom would want us to fight for her. She wouldn't want to be kept like that. Mom's a fighter, she's not going to give up, and we can't either." Tears splashed down her cheeks and she rested her head on Paul's shoulder. "Dad?"

"You're right." Paul kissed the top of her head.

Doctor Tobias looked to Kain, who said, "It's their decision. I should have explained who was here first. Her husbands: Paul and Mathew. Children: Paris and London. The rest of us are here for Paris and moral support.

The doctor nodded before he cleared his throat. "I'd like to run some additional tests on Mrs. Nelson, to check the cancer and what the treatment has done since her last scans. With your permission I'll do that, then we'll gather and go over what I find before I need a final decision. It should take a few hours before all the tests are complete. You'll have time to talk it over, I'll also be around to answer any questions you might have."

"Thank you, Doctor Tobias." Mathew held out his hand to him. When the doctor left he turned back to Kain. "Thank you too for bringing him here."

She slipped away from Paul's arm and went to stand in front of Kain. "You're an amazing man. I can't believe how lucky I am to call you mine."

Chapter Thirteen

Paris stepped into her quarters at home, her men fanning out around her, and London stewing across the hall. They had been sent home to rest while the tests where done and her dads stayed by her mother's bedside. She had been reluctant to leave but when Cody had vowed to throw her over his shoulder and carry her from the hospital she voiced opposition but eventually gave in. Her sweet men hadn't left her side since they arrived and for once she truly understood what her mother had tried to tell her for years. There was nothing better than the love of good men.

"Shower or sleep first?" Cody set her bags on the chair by her desk and turned to her.

"Neither, I think I'm going to run off my anxiety." She headed to the closet to get a workout outfit when Cody came up behind her and wrapped his arms around her.

"Oh, no you don't. We're under strict orders not to let you out of our sight."

"Then you can join me. Either way I'm not tired and I can't just sit around here doing nothing."

He plucked her off the floor as if she weighed nothing. "I can think of other ways for you to burn off this fretfulness."

She glanced to Aiden and Kain for help, only to find them smirking as they slipped out the door. "Hey!"

"You need this." Kain smirked before leaving them alone.

"He's right, we both need this." Cody strolled toward her bedroom with her in his arms. "Let us just exist for an hour than we'll get ready and go back to the hospital."

She stopped fighting him and relaxed into his embrace. "What did you have in mind?"

"I'm going to sit you on the sofa and I want you to stay there. I'm going to build a quick fire and then you're mine." He placed her on the bed and hesitated a moment as if he thought she'd hop off.

"I'm already yours."

Taking the logs from beside the fireplace, he quickly built the fire, warming the room almost instantly. "Your heart might be mine, as my heart is yours. Now I'm going to claim your body."

"My sweet Cody…I need you."

He crossed the space to her quickly. "Lie back."

She did as he asked, leaning back against the throw pillows as he came to sit beside her. "Before we received the call about your mother I had a romantic evening planned. It wasn't about getting you into bed, but just to show you how much I care for you. When Aiden called my cell and told me to get the plane ready the one thing I wanted was to be by your side, to hold you. I knew what needed to be done, but I couldn't help but be jealous of Aiden and Kain for being with you in your time of need."

"You're with me now and that's what matters. You were with me at the hospital and you'll be there for me in the future. I needed to get home and you saw to that, and that was something only you could do for me. For that I'll always be grateful." She reached up and ran her hand over his cheek, across his stubble and along his jawline before caressing down to his chin with her thumb.

"My sweet Cody, I love you."

"I love you, too," he whispered, nuzzling against her hand. "Now I want to show you how much you mean to me."

The fireplace crackled, sending sparks up the chimney and helping to create a romantic moment. She needed this. She needed him, not just to take her mind off what was going on, but because she loved him. She couldn't deny what her mind and body craved, no more than she could deny her lungs air.

"Come here, I need you, Cody." She continued to caress his face. "Take my mind off everything else, relieve this burning desire within me and make me feel like a woman."

"Let me show you how desirable you are." He scooted as close to her hip as he could get and ran his fingers through her hair. "You're beautiful."

She felt her cheeks heat with embarrassment, but before she could say anything he closed the distance, claiming her lips. She tasted the saltiness from the buttered popcorn they had shared at the hospital. It had been one of the few things the vending machine had, and since they had missed dinner it was that or nothing. Wanting more of him, she let her tongue slip into his mouth and explore. He slipped his fingers beneath the hem of her sweater, gently pulling it up, breaking the kiss to tug it over her head.

The warmth from the fireplace hit her as he tossed the shirt aside. As she began to pull off his shirt, he stopped her.

"Paris…my own need has risen to a level that's hard to control, but I understand if you'd rather wait."

"I want you. That is one of the only things I'm sure about right now." Her fingers caressed his smooth stomach. "Though may I suggest the bed?"

"You're right, the bed would be better." He stood and scooped her into his arms.

"I can walk."

"Oh, love, I've seen you do that and I can't get enough of watching you move."

She chuckled and leaned her head against his chest, letting him carry her the short walk to the bed. She wrapped her arms around his neck. "So the sway of my hips turns you on?"

"One of many things." He laid her in the center of the large bed, with the burgundy bedspread and silver and black pillows mounted in front of the black rod iron headboard. "You're beautiful, surrounded by all these pillows. Though if we're going to sleep here with you, some of them might need to go."

He wasted no time stripping his clothes off and she suspected he was also overcome by yearning. She tried to memorize the sight of him naked before he crawled onto the bed next to her and went to work on the buttons of her jeans. Her fingers played over his perfect abs, the bulging muscles in his arms. None of his muscles were from time in a gym, they'd been built due to manual labor, lifting hay. Her body heated at the thought of having her way with him in the barn. It would give him a good memory of the ranch, instead of making him think of what happened with his mother. She made a mental note to do it when they made it back to Wyoming.

He kissed her stomach right above the hem of her jeans, drawing her back from her thoughts and into the moment. She stared at him while she slid her hand down his chest until she found his shaft. She wrapped her fingers around it and rubbed down the length, painstakingly slow. "I love when you look at me like that."

"Like what?" His voice was hitched up a notch.

"Like I complete you. Like I'm the woman you've looked for all your life."

"You are." At those two simple words her grip on his shaft loosened and he was able to slip away.

"Get back here," she ordered, unable to keep the smirk off her face.

"Later, now unhook your bra, I want to see all of you. Oh, what a beautiful sight that will be." A growl pushed its way up his throat when she didn't move.

"Damn, woman, you're gorgeous. Stop making a man wait." She didn't have time to respond before he claimed her mouth.

When the kiss ended, leaving her breathless, he whispered, "You won't take it off, then I'll work around it." He pushed her bra to the side as his lips feverishly claimed her nipple. His other hand went to the waistband of her jeans and pushed them down her legs. With them went her last shred of reservation.

"Please…" She reached out, her hand landing firmly on his chest, forcing him closer to her. His shaft pressed tight against her thigh. In his arms for the first time she felt safe and wanted. She ran her nails over his chest, her need riding her.

"I need you inside me. Please…"

He slipped his hand up her hip and moved to hover over her, angled between her spread thighs. He glided his shaft over her opening, pulling a moan from her. Slowly he pushed the length in, just a little at first as he worked his way inside her tight passage. Halfway in, he stopped, slid out, then gripped her hips and slammed his length into her, filling her completely.

She leaned back, grabbing the edge of the headboard, arching toward him. With every thrust, her eyes fluttered shut as a climax built within her. She sprung her eyes open again as he dipped his head and drew his tongue along each nipple, blowing gently on them.

"Faster." She lifted her hips to meet his as he pumped into her.

With each stroke he brought it up another level, slowly intensifying the tempo until she was ready to roll him over and do it herself. When her control was almost at its limit, his hips slammed into her as she met each thrust.

"My sweet Paris, come for me."

Minutes later, an orgasm coursed through her, and her body arched into his.

He buried his head in her shoulder, growling her name as his own release followed. Kissing her neck, he stayed buried deep within her. "I love you." He kissed a line along her neck, working his way to her ear.

"If you keep doing that, I'm going to be ready for round two."

As if agreeing, his shaft twitched, hardening against the walls of her core. "I think we can arrange that."

"Umm." She moaned, teasing her fingers along his sides. "I need a shower before we go back to the hospital."

"Cuddle session first…maybe a little sleep." His voice suddenly as heavy as her eyelids felt. He slipped off her to cuddle next to her as their breathing began to return to normal. In his embrace she was contented, safe, but most importantly loved. Finding Aiden, Kain, and Cody was more than she could have ever asked for.

Paris's eyelids fluttered open to find herself alone in bed, the soft male voices from the sofa bringing her fully awake. Her men were watching over her as she slept. She rolled over on her side, propping her head up with her elbow. "Why didn't you guys wake me earlier?"

"You've been asleep less than an hour." Cody turned enough on the sofa to look back at her.

"That's it?" She rolled her neck. "It feels longer than that."

"You should try to get some more sleep. We can go to the other room if it would help," Kain suggested.

"I'm awake and I need a shower. Anyone want to join me?" She sat up in bed, letting the covers pool at her waist. After all there was nothing to be shy about now, they had all seen her naked.

"I thought I'd have to convince you to shower with me." Aiden stretched his long legs out and stood. "The others showered while you were sleeping so that just leaves me to clean you."

"I'm sure we can put the shower time to good use." She slid her legs out from under the covers and stood. "Then I want to get back to the hospital."

"Kain and I will find something in the kitchen to whip up and take with us for your dads."

"Thanks, Cody." She took a step toward him but halted. She hated to deny herself a simple touch and kiss with Cody, but she had Aiden waiting.

"Go to him." Aiden seemed to understand. Instead of making her feel guilty, he nodded to the bathroom. "I'll get the shower going. I know you'll join me when you're ready."

"Thank you." She watched him for a moment as he strolled toward the bathroom before she went to Cody.

"What's wrong, love?" Cody placed his hands on her hips and drew her close to his chest.

"I just wanted to feel your arms around me. You're so thoughtful about those around you." She ran a finger down his jaw line, feeling the smoothness of a fresh shave under her touch. "Thank you."

"Woman, there's no reason to thank me. Now Aiden's waiting for you and when you're done, come downstairs. I'll have something for you to eat."

"A man who can cook and who insists on feeding me, I could get used to this." She rose up on her tippy-toes and kissed him.

When the kiss ended, he lightly smacked her ass. "Go on, we're wasting time."

"It's never wasted time with your loved ones." She smirked and stepped back.

Kain cleared his throat as she started toward the bathroom. "What I don't get a kiss?" His eyes twinkled with amusement.

"You're wicked, but get over here." The kiss was light, but enough to make her want to throw him on the bed. When he finally pulled back, she was breathless. "Damn."

"A promise of what I've got for you later."

She watched them leave before she made a move toward the bathroom. They might have been using their bodies as a way to distract her and keep her thoughts from turning back to the pending test, but she couldn't complain. She needed something to pass the time and sex was better than staring at the hospital's white walls for hours.

Her desire level rising, she turned on her heels and headed to where she knew Aiden was waiting for her. She had barely stepped into the bathroom when she got the first glimpse of what was waiting for her.

She slipped into the shower without waiting for an invitation. He stood with his back to her under the raining showerheads, soap running down his body. Even though he didn't turn around, his back muscles tightened. For a moment, she stood there enjoying the way the soap bubbles slid down his body, before racing down the drain. Finally she stepped closer, giving into her temptation, running her hands up his slippery back.

"I knew you'd join me." He leaned back, letting the water run through his hair. "Damn, you get more beautiful each day." He advanced on her and pushed her against the cool tile, grasping her wrists with one hand and holding them hostage above her head.

"Funny, I was thinking something similar…though more manly. I don't know how I got so lucky to find the three of you, but it's more than I could have hoped for. You've invaded every thought I have. You keep my body on edge."

"Let me take the edge off you." He crushed his mouth to hers, and slid his hand between her legs. He worked his thumb and forefinger against her nub to drive the pleasure from her. Heat erupted against his touch, radiating in tingling waves outward, weakening her legs. If he hadn't been bracing her against the wall, she'd have slid down onto the floor. Fierce desire rose within her.

"Take me," she murmured against his mouth, holding onto him as wild delight streamed through her.

He grazed her lower lip with his teeth and pulled his hand away. She cried out in frustration, but he ignored her demands. Gripping her hips, he lifted her and spread her thighs before he drove into her with one powerful thrust. She moaned and twined her arms around his shoulders as he withdrew and thrust into her again, deeper, harder, his pumping almost savage as he revealed some of the beast within. The water pummeled from the outside while his pounding sparked sensations inside of her she'd never experienced.

He left her mouth, feathering kisses along her collarbone. She held onto his shoulders as every pump of his hips sent pulses of pleasure exploding through her. She tightened her legs around him as he groaned and shoved himself deeper into her. The pressure built within her until her body trembled and another orgasm rushed upon her. She held onto him as he slammed home in a frenzy. A climax tour through her with such force her world came apart at the seams, her inner muscles clenching around him as he continued to drive into her.

His climax burst through as a second tsunami shattered her world. She shook with the force of it. This man utterly devastated her.

The water turned cold and he shut it off, sliding free of her slowly and reluctantly. Her mind was almost numb, raw sensation skittering through her. With loving tenderness, he used a large towel to dry her off.

"Beautiful..." When she didn't look up at him, he used his index finger to tip her head. "You okay?"

She couldn't blink the tears away, instead she wrapped her arm around him, burying her face in his chest. "What if I lose one of you?"

"Shh, love, that's not going to happen." He wrapped the towel around her shoulders and held her tight.

"If Mom's cancer has taught me anything it's that we're never guaranteed tomorrow." She wrapped her arms around his waist. "I don't know how I could live without each of you."

"I know, love, but it's going to be okay. We've got many years together before anything will happen to any of us."

"Each of you are so different than the other but somehow you've come together to be everything I wanted in my husbands. Cody is the sensitive, caring, and romantic one. Kain, my sexy cowboy is strong, protective, resourceful, yet has a side he keeps hidden from others that I've gotten to see and explore. Then there's you." She leaned back to look at him. "My football player turned businessman. Just like me, you have a work ethic that drives others mad. Still you find time for me and the others. You have depths I have yet to explore, but I have a feeling you're as much of a romantic as our Cody." She paused and leaned back a little farther. "Until now, I hadn't realized it but..."

"What, beautiful?"

"Somehow you've taken the lead. Kain and Cody both look up to you. Even when it came to me, you were the first one to claim my body, and only then did the others follow suit. Cody might be shy compared to you and Kain, but he's a man of his own right. Then there's Kain who almost seems like he should be in charge. He's got the authority in his tone. He's the one who reached out to the company for help finding a woman. Yet he looks to you to guide things along more than Cody does. How did you manage to get two strong men to follow your lead without a sexual lure?"

Aiden leaned away from her, his muscles tightened under her embrace. "Are you claiming that the guys and I have kept a sexual relationship from you? Because I'm sorry to disappoint you but all we share is friendship. We have a brotherly bond, you might even say we love each other, but there's nothing sexual about it."

"I didn't mean to imply anything. Only what I've seen. I think the four of us work so well because you've already worked this out between the three of you before you found me. This saved us from having a struggle over dominance." She lightly hooked her feet behind his knees to draw him closer to her. "You, my gorgeous man, are the leader of our little group. Did you realize that?" She took in his stunned expression and 'smirked. "You never knew."

"I guess I didn't, we've just always been together, working together. We'll continue to work together to make you happy and to make sure you have everything you want."

"The three of you are all I want." She leaned in closer, drawing their lips together. Her lips brushed against his and she whispered, "I love you, Aiden."

Chapter Fourteen

By the time Paris and the others arrived back at the hospital, things were buzzing. Family and friends rushing to see people, nurses and doctors busy at work, even with all the activity it was hard to forget what this place represented. The awful stench of illness and ammonia enveloped her as they made their way down the long corridor. The smell stole the breath from her lungs. Hospitals were the one place she always hated. The stench never seemed to disappear, and hidden within the walls were people breathing their last.

Kain had his arm around her waist, his fingers teasing over her hip as they walked. "Deep breaths."

"Easier said than done." She felt like she couldn't get enough air and black dots danced in her vision.

"Do you want to stop for a moment?" When she shook his head, he tightened his embrace, pulling her a little snugger against his body. "I've got you, now just breathe."

"Are you okay?" Aiden came up to her other side and took her hand into his.

"I'm just freaking out about whatever it was Doctor Tobias found that made him call us back to the hospital an hour before the scheduled meeting...that's all." She tried to make light of it as her heart tried to beat its way out of her chest.

"It's going to be okay. Remember, whatever the reason, it might not be bad, and we're here by your side." Aiden reassured her.

"You're making a scene, Paris, let's go," London bitched.

"Why don't you go on ahead if you're in a rush?" Kain's body tensed. "Doctor Tobias won't be there for another ten minutes."

Aiden stopped and turned to London who had been lagging behind them. "Your problem has been with me since I arrived, but your sister doesn't need this. Instead of this ill directed anger, you should be thinking about your mother. Let us worry about Paris."

"How am I supposed to stand by and watch as you hurt her? When you leave I'll be the one left behind to help her pick up the pieces."

She shook out of Kain's embrace and spun around. "London, I've had enough." The tears she had been holding back forced their way down her face. "I love you, but I just can't take this. Right now I don't honestly care that you don't like Aiden. I love him and that's what should matter to you. If you can't support my decision to be with him, that's your choice, however I can't stand for your hostile attitude. Right now the whole family needs to be joined together for Mom's sake and that includes Aiden, Kain, and Cody. Please, little brother, I'm not asking for you to be happy for me, just stop being so angry at least until we get Mom better. Then if you want to rant and rave, have at it." She tried to keep her voice low, but she could see people glancing in their direction.

Mathew, who had joined them sometime during her rant, cleared his throat. "I had hoped after sending you home with them, you'd have worked out whatever issue you have with Mr. Dalton. Since you haven't, I'm going to ask you to keep your distance. Right now we're dealing with enough and our focus needs to be on Mom. We'll deal with your grievance in time. Now, Doctor Tobias will be joining us shortly so can we please act like a family that gets alone instead of having these discussions in the hallway?"

London brushed past them and into the critical care waiting room when Dad turned to her. "Paris, I'm sorry you have to deal with this. He'll come around if you give him some time."

"Right now I don't care." Even as she said the words, she knew it was a lie. "Right now I'm focused on Mom, the company, and them." She glanced at her men before turning her attention back to Dad. "Any change with Mom?"

"We haven't been able to see her until a few minutes ago since they were doing the tests. But I have to tell you I received a heads-up from a journalist friend of mine that the media has gotten hold of this. They know she's been admitted and within the hour they'll be outside." Mathew glanced to Aiden. "It's only going to make it worse that you and the others are here. If you want to slip out before the madness starts, now's your chance."

"Absolutely not. We're here with Paris and you all the way. I'll apologize in advance if my former career brings any additional media attention to you and your family at this time, but we'll stay with her unless she asks us to leave." Aiden looked down at her.

"I'd never ask that." She leaned her head against his chest.

"Good." Mathew nodded. "I'm glad to see my little girl has men who will stand by her side instead of running off when things get tough."

"Oh, Dad, did you really think I'd choose anyone but the best? After all, I had good role models, and my men have the same outstanding qualities my fathers have."

"Guys…" Paul stood just down the hall, ushering them along. "I'd like a few minutes to talk this over as a family before Doctor Tobias joins us."

Outside the waiting room, Kain touched her arm. "Maybe we should wait out here."

"Oh no." Mathew shook his head. "You're part of this dysfunctional family now, and you brought Doctor Tobias to us."

"He's right and I want you with me." When she still saw a hint of hesitation in his eyes, she stepped closer to Kain and laid her hand on his chest. "Please."

"When you put it like that, how could I deny you?"

Her cowboy leaned down toward her. "We'll always be at your side. Don't doubt that. I only thought you and your family would like to discuss this and make a decision without the three of us hanging around, especially with London's current attitude toward the situation."

"He'll get over it, or he won't. I'm not letting it change things for me. For the first time in longer than I can remember I'm truly happy. You three make me happy. I have something besides work. Don't get me wrong, I love my work but it makes it all the more worth it to know I have you guys waiting for me at the end of the day."

Inside the waiting room, Paul and London were already sitting at the only table. Mathew went to take the seat next to Paul, leaving four empty seats for them. Feeling only slightly guilty, she took the seat next to Mathew and let her men work out who sat to her right. Kain, Aiden, and Cody sat in that order so that Kain was next to her and Cody sat next to London. She wasn't completely sure it was the best idea to have Cody there, but before she could give it more thought Paul leaned forward placing his hands on the table.

"Mathew and I have been discussing the situation with Mom, as well as looking over the study that is ongoing with this drug. We agreed not to make a final decision until we know where the new tests stand. However, we have an idea which way we're leaning. We also have some additional questions for Doctor Tobias. The question is, have you given it more thought? Paris, let's start with you."

"As I said before, I know Mom would want us to fight for her. From what the doctor said before her chances of a recovery with this drug are stronger than without. I think we've got to trust him and do it. If it was me in that bed, I would hope you'd do the same for me. I don't want to be left unconscious as life passes me by. If I'm alive then I want to be enjoying it with my family, otherwise…pull the plug."

"We're not talking about you," London snapped.

She forced a deep breath into her lungs and held onto the chair to keep from climbing over the table to smack him. "Any idea where I got it from? Mom! She's the one who taught me the value of life. Do you honestly think Mom wants that?"

"It's better than losing her."

"How?" She leaned forward in her chair. "If she can't be an active part of our lives, how is this better? What about Dads? Don't they deserve to have their wife home with them?"

"Paris." Mathew laid his hand on her shoulder.

She turned her head so quickly she felt her muscles cry out in pain. "What? You agree with him?"

"No, but London is scared of the alternative. It's understandable. We all are." Tears glistened in Mathew's eyes. "I don't want to lose my wife. She's the glue that keeps us all together, the reason I get up in the morning. There's nothing better than opening my eyes and having her face the first thing I see."

"Maybe she'll come back to us on her own. Maybe she doesn't need this drug. As you said, Paris, Mom's a fighter," London tried to reason.

"The longer she's in the coma the less likely that is," Paul pointed out. "If this continues much longer there could be more damage done from the coma itself. Not to mention that she's not undergoing her treatments."

"You've already decided to do it, haven't you?" London pushed his chair back and stood. "Why have us gather around if we have no say in what happens?"

"I said when we sat down that Mathew and I already had a direction we're leaning toward. Yes, if the tests come back that she's a candidate and our questions are answered as we expect, then we've decided to do it. As for why we want your thoughts on it, you're both adults and our children, your opinion matters." Paul eyed London and added, "Though I will say I had expected you to handle this whole situation better. You're not acting like an adult, but a spoiled child. I know you're upset about Paris's men, but that's no reason for this."

"I'm looking out for my sister!" London raged, glaring at Mathew. "Weren't you just demanding that she come home because there's danger surrounding Kain because of that baseball player?"

"We have taken precautions to ensure Paris is safe from Kings." Kain turned to look at London, who was now pacing behind the table. "Kings might be an ass and after me, but he wouldn't harm innocent bystanders."

"You can't guarantee that."

"There have been attacks on all of us *before* Kain came into my life." She pushed back the chair and stood. "Remember a year ago? Those protestors attacked, and Schwartz ended up totaling the SUV trying to get us out of there safely. This is nothing new. That wasn't the first time and I'm sure it won't be the last time I'm a victim because of the lifestyle I choose to live."

"Is this a bad time?" a voice interrupted.

She turned to see Doctor Tobias standing there, files in hand.

"No, Doctor. Please come in and tell us what you discovered about my mother's condition."

He grabbed a chair that was against the wall and brought it to sit between her and Mathew. "As you know I've ran a new batch of tests, some which they already ran and others they hadn't. Every test from the simplest blood work, to additional scans to see where the cancer is and how advanced it is. I have some good news and bad news. The good news is Mrs. Nelson would be a perfect candidate for this drug."

"The bad news?" Mathew asked.

"Her white blood cells are elevated, as if she's fighting off some type of infection. I've ordered the blood work again, as well as a brain scan."

142

"Couldn't the white blood cells be high because of the cancer? I thought they were high last time as well, weren't they?" Paul looked to Mathew for confirmation, who nodded.

"This brings me to the main reason I've called you together." Doctor Tobias glanced at Kain, a huge smile etched over his face before he turned back to Mathew and Paul. "The cancer is gone."

"What?" Paris couldn't dam the tears up as they began falling freely down her face. "That can't be? Doctor Vander said—"

"I've read all of his files, and I've looked at the tests they ran before her treatments began as well as the ones done two weeks ago. It's truly remarkable, but the cancer is gone." Doctor Tobias pulled two x-rays out of the folder that sat before him. "This was two weeks ago and this…this was taken less than an hour ago."

Paris blinked and tried to take it in while her mind screamed it was a dream. She couldn't process it. For weeks the whole family had started to prepare themselves for a huge loss. Even though Mom was still alive, Paris knew she had already started to grieve for what they all thought was the inevitable. After finding out Mom was going to live, her chest was tightening and she couldn't breathe.

"I need to see her, please…"

Kain wrapped his arm around her, drawing her close to his body. She hadn't noticed Aiden and Cody get up from their chairs but suddenly they were behind her, their hands on her shoulders.

An hour later Paris was sitting by her mother's bedside, still in shock. The whole family had eaten, thanks to Cody who had brought food from the house since they were rushed back to the hospital. The additional tests had all come back clean, and now they were just gathered around her bedside to see if the drugs would work. The only one missing was London, who'd decided he needed fresh air. She suspected he was still fuming over the whole situation with Aiden, along with the family siding against him on this treatment.

Her baby brother needed a wake-up call. Only a few weeks ago she had thought he was finally growing up, no longer that selfish partier he had been. Now she realized she couldn't have been more wrong. He might not have been out every night at the clubs, or showing his friends or clients a good time, but his attitude hadn't changed. If anything it had gotten worse. Right now, everyone was more concerned about Mom than London's attitude, but it wouldn't be long before someone had it out with him. She hoped it wouldn't be her because she couldn't take much more before she snapped.

"It could be hours before anything changes. It's pointless for everyone to sit around here watching," Paul reasoned.

"I'm not going anywhere." She barely took her gaze away from her mother. "This is the first chance I've been able to see Mom since I arrived."

"I need some fresh air, and I have to chat with that son of ours." Paul patted Mathew's shoulder. "Will you be okay?"

He nodded. "Go ahead. I'll call your cell if she starts to wake up." After Paul left, Mathew turned in his seat to look at her. "London is scared, upset...let's face it, even with everything that has happened and the responsibilities the two of you have taken on, he has been unwilling to grow up. His immaturity is showing in his current attitude. But he's still your brother—"

"Dad, I know he is or I wouldn't have put up with his shit."

"He's scared to lose Mom."

She took a deep breath and reminded herself to keep her voice low. "What, I'm not?"

"I only meant that he's dealing with it in his own way. He's also thinks he's watching out for you by trying to protect you from Aiden." He held up his hand to stop her before she could interrupt. "I know his protection is misguided to say the least. I'm just asking that you cut him a little more slack. Paul has gone to talk to him and maybe he can get him to see some sense."

"You and Dad don't need to worry about this. London and I will eventually work this out. I'm sure he's upset I didn't tell him I had been going to see Aiden." She glanced to Aiden and her other two men who had given the security guards a break to grab something to eat, while they watched over the family. They stood outside the room, the wall of windows between them so they were never out of sight. "That day you called to tell me about that ball player who had a grudge against Kain…I had made plans to tell London everything when I arrived back home, but things got busy. He had something with work come up, my work, Mom, and traveling back and forth each week. It all got away from me. I wanted to tell him but the time never seemed right."

"You're not the only one at fault there. We all kept it from him."

"I just wish he'd quit with this crap before the media gets hold of this." She hadn't thought about it when she agreed to have them come home with her, all she had done was give in to her desire to have them by her side, but now she was thinking clearly and it hit her. "Oh, Dad, I didn't think…"

"What's wrong? Not happy with them? They seem completely devoted to you." He turned to look through the glass doors to where the men stood.

"No, it's not them. I love them. I didn't think what bringing them home would cause. Since the media has already got hold of Mom's condition, they're going to be waiting for us. Once they see me walk out of there with them, embraced by one or more of them, they'll know and it will be all over the papers by morning."

"You're used to being the center of gossip. For years you've had to deal with it, because of us, the company. This isn't any different."

"It is because my commitment to them is going to overshadow the real reason we're at the hospital. Mom."

"Now, I think that might be the first bright spot of things. We've worked hard to keep her condition quiet, so if we can continue it then that's great. When it breaks, maybe it won't be the center of the attention. Instead, you and your men will be."

She shook her head. "Thanks, Dad, now I feel like I'm being used. This isn't a time to be—"

"Paris, do you love them?"

"What? I just said I did." She let go of Mom's hand and turned in her chair to look at him.

"If you love them like I think you do, then it doesn't matter when they come into the family, just that they have. Love sometimes comes to us at what we think is the worst time, but is actually the best, otherwise we might not have been able to get through the situation as well as we would have without that love. Paris, don't doubt that you found your men when you needed them the most and when they needed you the most. It's destiny, and I'm glad to see you have people who care about you and who you care about."

"The best thing about this family is I always have people I love with me, no matter what. You're the best dad a girl could ask for." She reached across to take his hand.

"Don't let Paul hear you say that."

"You're both amazing, but where Dad is there for comfort, you're always there with the right words. The best of both."

All of a sudden, a rough voice whispered and Paris realized it was her mother.

"They're…all mine," she rasped.

Her stomach roiled; she hadn't been sure this would work and now Amy was awake. She wanted to wrap her arms around Mom, but instead she was frozen to the spot. Dad leaned forward, practically climbing into the bed next to her, making Paris feel like she was invading a private moment.

"Amy…my sweet Amy!" He kissed her and hugged her to him.

"I'll call the family." She rose from the chair to tell her men the good news.

"Paris, is everything okay?" Kain asked as she came out of the room, unable to look away from her parents.

"Mom…Mom's awake!"

"Give me your phone." Cody held out his hand. "I'll call Paul and London."

She slipped the phone out of the pocket of her jeans and handed it to him. "Dad went to find London. They should be together."

With Cody stepping away from them to make the calls, she turned back to Kain. "You…this is all because of you."

"Not me, darling. Doctor Tobias did this, I just brought him here." He wrapped his arm around her shoulders. "I'm glad your mother is doing better."

"We both are." Aiden placed a hand on her shoulder.

Words couldn't express what she was feeling at the moment. She wasn't even sure she could explain it if she had to. She was numb, yet ecstatic that her mother's health had begun to improve. She needed to let this all sink in, and then she was going to celebrate. Celebrate with her men.

Chapter Fifteen

Over the last few hours, Paris and her family had mostly stood around doing nothing, while Doctor Tobias ordered test after test to see how the experimental drug had affected her system. No one wanted to tell Amy about the remission until they had the last of the test results in.

"Excuse me."

Paris turned to find a nurse in pale blue scrubs standing in the door of the waiting room.

"Yes?"

"Mrs. Nelson has asked for her daughter."

"That's me." She nearly jumped off the sofa.

"She's back from her tests but Doctor Tobias has orders that she rests for a bit before everyone is allowed back there. One person may remain with her. Umm….one of the…Mr. Nelson is back there now and has agreed to step out while she speaks with you." The poor woman looked completely confused on how to handle the situation of two husbands.

"Cody, go with her," Mathew ordered. "The hospital and security guards have been doing a good job at keeping the media out but Paris needs someone with her."

"Dad."

"He's right," Aiden said. "Just to be safe. Cody's the best one to go with you because he blends better than Kain or I."

"Come on, love, let's not keep your mom waiting." Cody slipped his hand into hers. "I'd never argue with them because they think they're always right."

"That's because we are," Kain added before they made it to the door.

"Plus it gives me time with my favorite person."

"My mom?" She teased.

He squeezed her hand. "You, love, are the only woman I have eyes for." He glanced out the hall and nodded before allowing her into the hallway. "I'll spend the rest of my life proving that to you."

"You're already doing that." She wanted to lean in to kiss his cheek, to let him know how much she appreciated everything he had done for her, but the nurse stepped out from one of the rooms as they entered the critical care wing and eyed them both.

"I thought I explained the doctor's orders are one at a time while she rests."

"I'm accompanying Miss Nelson as her security guard. We're not taking any chances with the media lurking around. I'll be waiting in the hallway with her father while she visits her mother," Cody explained.

When the nurse started to voice her opposition, Paris added, "If you have an issue with this arrangement please speak with your supervisor. My father, Mathew Nelson, has already worked things out with him." She looked down at the nurse's badge. "Ms. Chase, I'm sure you've watched the news, so you know who my family is. You'll understand the need for security. We never go anywhere alone. It's security for us as well as for others. Now unless you wish to make a big deal of this and get your supervisor involved, I suggest you go about your business and we will too."

Paris might have been able to phrase it better, but in the end it got the nurse scurrying off to do whatever task she had been neglecting, and allowed them to continue down the hall toward her mother's room. The lack of sleep was beginning to take a toll on her and she just didn't have the patience for anything at the moment.

"Aren't you a feisty kitten."

"Tired, sorry." She paused as a yawn overcame her. "Normally, I'm only feisty when I need to defend my family. We've been through a lot and we're close…well, at least most of the time. This issue with London is new and has already worn thin."

"He's a scared and confused kid. I've talked to him a little and it's clear he does care for you. Right now he's lashing out at you and our situation instead of facing what's really got him scared…your mom's condition. Give him time, I think he'll come around."

"If he doesn't, then we've got some issues." They stood in front of the door to Amy's room. "Mom doesn't need to know about this, but if she comes home to this tension in her condition…"

"Love, let's not borrow troubles we don't have yet. Maybe he'll come around before then. Go on in there and we'll deal with London later."

"Thank you." She quickly squeezed his hand before letting it go.

When Paul saw her, he rose from the bed and came to her by the door. "Stay with her as long as you want but make sure she rests."

"Quit giving orders, Paul." Mom held her hand out. "Come here, Paris."

She went, sat down, and took Mom's hand in hers. "Dad's right, you should be resting."

"In a bit. I caught a glimpse of your men earlier and wanted to talk to you about them. We haven't been able to talk lately, mostly because I've been so tired. What's happening with you and these men? Are things getting serious? I'd hope so since you brought them home."

"Oh, Mom, this girl chat can wait." At her mother's glare, she scooted the chair closer to the bed. "Dad called Aiden because I had left my cell phone downstairs when I went to the lookout room with Kain. After they knew the situation, they wouldn't take no for an answer and honestly I wanted them by my side since I didn't know what I was coming home to."

"You love them?"

"Simple answer is yes. Long answer...it's like a fire of desire and need burning within me. I want to have them by my side, always. It's unlike anything I've ever experienced. When they're not with me there's a piece of me missing and I long to find it."

Mom's lips curled up into a bright smile. "That, my little girl, is love. It's what your dads and I wanted both our children to find. Now, what are you going to do with it?"

"What do you mean?"

"Are you going to marry those boys?" She pushed the button to make the bed go up farther.

"Mom...they haven't asked. We're just.....exploring each other's wants and needs."

"Bodies, too, I'm thinking...by the way you're looking at them."

"Mom!" Paris couldn't stop the heat from rushing to her cheeks. They were best friends, but they had never discussed sex before, and she wasn't sure she wanted to now.

"I'll take that as a yes." She glanced toward the door. "Paul's getting impatient and I can tell he's biting at the bit to get back in here. So, just one last question..."

"Why do I have a feeling I'm not going to like this?"

"If they asked you today, would you spend the rest of your life with them?"

Paris didn't even need to think about it. "Yes."

"Good. Then I don't want you sitting around this hospital. I've got Mathew and Paul; neither of them are going to be leaving my side. Go home, get some sleep, and spend time with your men." When Paris started to argue, Mom squeezed her hand. "I won't hear no. Listen to your sick mother and go home, even if it's just for a few hours. Paul said by morning I should be in a private room, so we won't have to worry about visiting hours, or the one person rule. Now go."

"Yes, Mom." She stood, leaned across the space and kissed her mother's cheek. "Mom, I'm glad you're doing better. I love you."

"I love you, too. Now I think you need to experience the love of good men." She winked at Paris.

She shook her head at her mother as she made her way from the room. A break from the hospital might be just want she needed, and she could get some sleep now that she wasn't stressed about her mother's condition. Or maybe she'd take Mom's advice and explore the perfect bodies of her men.

Paris stepped out of the steaming hot Jacuzzi tub. The only thing she could hear in the distance were the voices of her men, chatting in her bedroom. With her fathers still at the hospital, and no one sure of where London had disappeared to, the rest of the house was quiet. She had left messages for her brother to call her. She promised her mother she'd spend time with her men, but she had also wanted to see if she could make any progress with her brother. The tension between them wasn't going to go away.

She slipped into a pair of black yoga pants and a pink tank top before running the comb through her wet hair. She took her time, giving herself a little longer to get her thoughts together before she went to find her men. They didn't need to see the worry in her eyes; they were already concerned enough about her.

"Darling, you're stressing yourself again." Kain came up behind her and slid his arms around her waist. "The whole point of the hot bath and none of us joining you—which I might say was a difficult task—was so you could relax. Let the water ease away some of the tension of the day. Now here you are buying trouble before it happens. If my guess is right, your thoughts are either on London or Kings."

She hadn't considered the whole situation with Kings, but now that he'd mentioned it, she realized it was in the back of her mind after all. "Why hasn't Kings come after you?"

"That, darling, I couldn't answer. He's made no secret of the fact he's pissed and blames me. Maybe he realizes that if he comes after me he'll either end up dead or back in prison. Sometimes vengeance isn't worth the cost." He placed a line of gentle kisses down the side of her face. "Now, darling, would you like to tell me what's really on your mind?"

"I was thinking about London. He took off after he saw Mom and no one has seen him since. How long does someone need to get fresh air?"

"He's a big boy and he'll come back when he's ready. He has a lot he needs to work through I'm sure. Now, come out here and we'll make you forget all about this."

She turned in his arms so her chest was pressed against him. "That sounds good."

He cupped her butt, lifted her, and she wrapped her legs around his waist. "Darling, you have too many clothes on. You should have come out naked."

"If the three of you had your way, you'd have me naked all the time," she teased.

"Not all the time but most of it, I could get used to that." He stepped away from the bathroom counter, carrying her toward the bedroom.

"It's about time you brought her out here." Aiden was stretched on the bed, naked, only the sheet hiding his manhood from view.

"What do we have here?" She raised an eyebrow at Aiden as Kain placed her on the mattress.

"I thought it was time we worked together to show you what we have to offer." He glanced up at Kain. "You should have got in there earlier. Now we'll have to undress her."

"Umm, undressing her is like unwrapping a Christmas gift you've waited your whole life for." Kain stripped out of his clothes and climbed onto the bed on her other side.

Not willing to wait any longer, she leaned toward Aiden and claimed his mouth. Diving her tongue between his lips, she was met with the spiciness of coffee, edged with hints of vanilla. The taste of him drew her in, wanting more until she was straddling his waist. Her tongue danced around his until she sucked his bottom lip between her teeth, and nipped gently.

"If you're working together, where's Cody?"

"Cody..." Hesitation and need edged his mumbling, while he slid his hands under her tank top.

"He'll join us." Kain ran his hands along her hips, his naked body pressed against her side.

"We should wait," she whispered as he kissed along the nape of her neck.

"He's coming," Kain confirmed once again. "Don't think you'll miss out on anything from us this time."

She nodded, sliding her fingers along the contours of his chest. "Then don't stop."

"I've been hoping to hear those words all day." Aiden pulled the tank top over her head and tossed it to the floor, revealing her naked breasts. The cool air swooshed over her and her nipples hardened into little buds. He shot her a smirk and lowered his head to claim one of her nipples. Sucking it between his lips, he let his teeth graze over it.

Meanwhile Kain slipped lower on the bed, hooking his fingers into the waistband of her pants and slipping them down her legs. A growl rose from deep within him. The passion running through her veins had taken control, forcing her to speed the pace. She wanted them. *Needed* was a better way to describe the desire tearing through her. She arched her body toward Aiden and ran her hands through Kain's hair.

She slid her hand down Aiden's chest, until his already growing shaft met her hand, and she wrapped her fingers around it. "Looks like someone's ready." Teasingly, she drew her nails down the length. Her body craved his touch, to feel his hands on her skin.

"I'll always be ready for you." He kissed a path down her neck, letting his warm breath caress her skin. Sensations collided and threatened to overwhelm her when he teased her nipples.

"You two couldn't wait until after I talked to the new guards downstairs?" Cody bitched as he strolled toward the bed, stripping as he moved.

Aiden let her nipple slip from his lips, his mouth hovering just over it. "If you'd have taken much longer you'd have missed all the action."

She reached out. "Join us."

Cody pulled off his jeans and tossed them at the edge of the huge bed. He stood there a moment as her gaze traveled over his body. "Do you like what you see?" he teased, watching her devour him with her eyes.

"Oh, yes!" She nodded, wanting to run her hands over his chest. Where Aiden was toned, Cody was beyond that; his body was carved out of stone, every muscle well defined. All the hours lifting the hay and attending to the horses. Even working the land had left him with a warm golden tan all over his body, that neither of her other men could compare to. "Come to me."

With a heated gaze, he joined them on the bed, nestling himself on the opposite side of her. With Aiden and Cody on either side of her, and Kain at her waist, she was surrounded by handsome naked men, making her a tiny bit self-conscious.

"I want you to lie back and enjoy. Let us do all the work," Aiden whispered, his mouth on her earlobe, gently tugging it with his teeth.

"Don't tease, I want each of you now." She reached out, her hand landing firmly on Cody's chest until he lowered closer into her. His shaft pressed tight against her thigh. They had her captive between their bodies, making her feel safe and wanted. In that moment all her fears were gone.

Kain slid on top of her, his bulky frame hovering above her as he stared down at her, desire burning in her eyes. He teased along the curves of her hips, the back of his hands brushing against the thighs of Aiden and Cody.

He blazed a hot, wet trail of kisses across her belly and stroked her thighs with his fingertips. With every touch, she arched her hips, demanding more. Nudging her legs farther apart, he delved inside her with his fingers and she met the teasing thrusts. A demanding moan tore through the air.

Passion drove fire through her. Their gazes stayed locked as he slipped lower on the bed. The trail of wicked kisses tingled over her thighs. He moved his fingers until his thumb was lightly teasing her bud before he replaced it with his mouth. Tiny nips and gentle licks flicked over her sweet spot until she wriggled beneath him. Her fingers locked in his hair, torn between pressing him closer and dragging him up.

"Kain!" She cried out, her legs twitching, her back arching as the release she needed surged forward. Her body felt torn between the three of them. While Kain worked his magic between her legs, Cody's mouth had claimed one of her nipples, and Aiden nibbled from her ear down to her neck.

Just as her release neared, Kain pulled back, his fingers replacing his mouth. "Not yet, darling, not yet." He continued to tease her with his thumb, forcing her to arch toward him, demanding more.

"I need you."

"Soon," Cody whispered, grazing over her hardened nipple with his teeth.

Aiden nibbled her lower lip and he pulled back enough to let her cries of frustration escape. He caressed every inch of her body, sending moans of ecstasy from her lips. For such a big man, he was incredibly tender, as though trying to memorize every curve of her body with his hands and mouth.

Heat soared through her blood, impatient and demanding. Her body always seemed to be on edge, needing their touches, and now she wanted them hard and fast. "I need one of you inside me. Now!"

Kain gently eased her legs open farther, giving him just enough room to position himself between them. He slipped on top of her, his bulky frame hovering above her as he stared down at her, desire burning in his eyes. His shaft teased along her entrance without entering as he watched her.

"Kain!" She reached up and grabbed his hips, determined to have him within her.

As if calling his name tore away the last shred of control he had, he drove into her with one powerful thrust. With it came a moan of both pleasure and pain. Even with the foreplay, she was still tight, her body wasn't ready for hard and fast yet, but he'd get her there. He gave her no time to catch her breath before he began rocking in and out, slow enough not to hurt her.

Cody scooted along the bed and knelt before her, his hard length jutting toward her. She took him into her mouth, working her way to the base. She used her hand to cup the end of the hard shaft, moving her mouth up and down the length, slowly at the tip. Cody groaned and reached to cup the back of her head. He allowed her to set the pace.

Trapped in the tempo of Cody and Kain's thrusts, she fought to find the perfect cadence to allow them to work together. Their rhythm quickly synced and she moaned, knowing they were being pleasured as one, rocking together in perfect harmony, as her ecstasy began to overwhelm her. While Aiden seemed content to wait his turn, he worked her nipple to ultimate hardness. Digging her nails into the backs of Cody's thighs, she held on to him as every pump sent pulses exploding through her. She came apart at the seams, her inner muscles clenching around Kain as he continued to drive his shaft into her.

Rapture engulfed her and Cody cried out his release. She writhed beneath Kain and Aiden's touches as she swallowed Cody's juices. Cody slipped from her lips and leaned against the headboard, his eyes closed. She tugged his hand, still reeling. She turned to Aiden, expecting to find him waiting, as she could feel the cord that reined in Aiden's desperation to touch her fraying. Instead, he shook his head. Before she could question it, Kain took hold of her hips, lifting her into the air to give him a deeper angle as he rocked deep within her.

With each pump his hips increased speed, driving the force deeper and faster. Finding a perfect rhythm, their bodies rocked back and forth, tension stretching her tighter as another climax began to climb upon her. He slammed home in a frenzy, shouting her name.

Without giving her time to recover, Aiden took Kain's place. He slid between her legs, his hands on her hips. "Open your eyes, beautiful."

As soon as she opened her eyes, he slid deep within her, and she moaned. He filled her slowly, inch by inch. Halfway in, he slid out before thrusting back in, filling her completely with his manhood. His strokes sparked feverish desire within her. She reached out to feel along the perfect contours of Kain's chest where he lay beside her. With Aiden between her legs, Cody nibbled her neck, his hand cupping her breast until his thumb found her nipple, and Kain collapsed next to her regaining his breath.

Aiden set his own tempo, not to be outdone by Kain. Taking it slower, making each stroke count. She dug her fingers into his back, clawing at him as a second orgasm neared. Her body clenched around his erection, which seemed to spark the fire within him and sent him pushing deeper and faster into her. He claimed her nipple with his mouth, pulling the bud between his teeth and applying just the perfect amount of pain to make it pleasurable. As if knowing she was close to a climax Aiden sped his pace, slamming into her until their hips hit off each other.

"Aiden!" She cried out as her orgasm tore through her. She clawed at his back as she pulled herself tight against him, meeting his thrusts. He pumped twice more and shouted her name, his own climax finding him. Eternity stretched on until he collapsed between her and Cody.

Her breath slowly returned to normal and she lay cradled between them. Her hand draped over Aiden's body so she could feel Cody. Everything went perfectly, and she almost suspected the men had choreographed how things would work, but she made a mental note to make sure they worked out something so it wasn't always Cody on the outside. If there was one thing, she knew about living this lifestyle it was never to show favoritism and always communicate.

For now, she was where she belonged—in their arms—and everything else could wait until later.

Chapter Sixteen

They must have dozed sometime after the lovemaking because the next thing Paris knew she was blinking to the sun in her eyes and her cell phone was vibrating its way to the edge of the nightstand. She started to sit up but found her men cuddled against her, nearly pinning her to the bed. Now that she was awake, the heat from their bodies almost became overwhelming.

"Where do you think you're going?" Aiden's eyelids popped open and he watched her, his arm tight around her waist.

"My phone." He grumbled something she wasn't able to make out before he reached behind him, grabbed the phone, and handed it to her. "Thank you."

"Is it Paul or Mathew?" He snuggled back against her, running his hand down her arm.

"No." She stared at the phone screen. London's name in bold letters left her unsure what she wanted to do. To call him back might only continue the fight, but she needed to know where he was, and eventually they had to work out their issues. Before she could make up her mind to return his call or just let it ride for the moment, her phone vibrated again, this time with a text message.

Coffee and scones. Join me. We need to talk.

"That could be a good step," Aiden whispered.

"Or the last thing I want this morning." She laid her head against his shoulder. "Either way I have to go take care of this."

"I wouldn't expect anything else from you." He glanced toward the others. "If you can slip out from their arms, we can let them sleep."

"You don't have to come downstairs and deal with this. I don't know what he has to say and if it's…"

He leaned up on his elbow and shook his head. "Part of his anger is because of me. You shouldn't have to deal with that alone. If you'd prefer Kain or Cody to go with you instead, I'll wake them, but your brother is pissed about the situation. There are extra guards downstairs that Cody met with last night but I would still feel better if one of us were with you."

She nodded because she'd prefer someone with her until she could judge London's mood. "Okay, but if he just wants to talk…"

"The guards and I will go to another room to give you privacy." He slipped out of the bed and held his hand out to her. "Come on, beautiful."

She took his hand and gently eased out of the bed, doing her best not to wake Kain or Cody. "Why additional guards? The house is secure. We've never had anyone make it through the walls of the compound."

"It's not for the house, but when we go out." He strolled over to the dresser and grabbed a fresh set of clothes out of his bag. "Beautiful, don't look at me like that, it's just a precaution. While you were in the bath last night, we found out Kings bought a ticket here a few days before we arrived. If Kings is pissed at Kain, for whatever happened, they'll work it out, but we're keeping you safe. No matter how pissed you might be about having the additional security guards."

She shrugged and tugged on a pair of jeans. "What's a few more guards, I've always had a security detail. My concern is, who are these guys? You can't normally flip through the yellow pages until you find them. Plus, the family keeps additional guards on a call list for when things get rough. I could have called them in."

"These are my men and they're the best." He tugged a royal blue sweater over his head and closed the distance between them. "Mathew also insisted Schwartz accompany you anytime you leave the house. He trusts this guy."

"But you don't? Even after you heard he saved my life."

"I haven't met him so I don't know. He was off because you were in Wyoming with us, but he should be here in an hour." He reached past her to grab his cell phone on the end table. "As for trusting him, I'll be able to tell you in a moment."

"What's that supposed to mean?" She fastened a black with white trim bra before she grabbed a warm green sweater, almost the colors of the leaves on the trees.

"I ran a check on him before you came out. Everything should be waiting for me." He hit a few buttons on the phone, mumbling to himself.

"You know if you wanted to check out Schwartz's past, I'd have shown you his file. We did the checks before we hired him."

He nodded, still not looking up from his phone. "Did you know that Schwartz has a sister with a drug problem? He's been raising his niece off and on for the last six months, but Friday the courts granted him permanent custody of the child."

"What?"

"I'll take that as a no." He held out the phone to her. "See for yourself."

She read the screen, scrolling down with her thumb to read the rest before looking up at him. "Why didn't he tell me?"

"You'll have to ask him."

She handed the phone back to him, grabbed her brush off the vanity, and dragged it through her long locks. After she spent as long as she could getting the tangles out, she set the brush aside. "I guess I can't put this off any longer."

"You could go back to bed and forget about it."

"No, London will wait there until I come down. He's persistent." With one last glance back to the bed and her sleeping men, she took a deep breath and strolled toward the door. She wasn't sure why she was so apprehensive, but every hair on the back of her neck stood, making her completely uneasy.

In the hall, Aiden placed his hand on the small of her back. She didn't think it was to guide her to the kitchen, but out of the need to touch. It had been something she had witnessed with her parents all her life; whenever they were together they'd share intimate touches every chance they got. Her men were the same way, but with three of them it seemed more important than ever so that they could each have their time with her.

"I had wondered if you'd come." London sat at the kitchen table. Even though it had taken her a little longer, the scones and coffee sat untouched. "Though I hadn't expected Aiden. I'll grab another coffee cup and plate."

"I'll just take some coffee and meet with the new guards in the other room." Aiden leaned down, placing his mouth next to her ear before whispering, "I'll just be in around the corner if you need me."

He grabbed the coffee London poured for him and stepped out, leaving Paris slightly stunned. She wasn't sure why he left as quickly as he did; maybe it had something to do with the dark circle under London's eyes, or his mellow attitude. Either way, Aiden must have believed there wouldn't be any fighting or he wouldn't have left so fast.

"London, what's this about?"

"Come sit." He poured them both coffee from the pot sitting in the middle of the table. "I thought we should talk."

She stepped closer to the table, though hesitation slowed her. "What about?"

"I've been an ass. It took Dad to knock some sense into me. When Paul came to find me pacing the sidewalk outside the hospital I was sure he was going to rip me a new one. Instead what he said made me realize the crap I had been doing to you, the guys, our family, and everyone else around us." He paused as she finally took the seat across from him. "I wanted you to know I'm sorry."

"What did Dad say in order to get you to see the error of your attitude?"

"Oh, this and that, but I was already coming to the conclusion that I was being a jerk before he found me. Aiden's past made me concerned for you, but if I just opened up my eyes I would have seen how much he cares for you."

"The media made it seem worse than it was. For some of the events he needed escorts, so he'd have a friend or a friend of a friend accompany him. He truly doesn't have a string of woman he's left discarded."

"Even if he did, it's not as though it was going to change things for you. I might have been blind to it before, but I can see the love you have for him. The only way would have been to let you learn for yourself, and then I'd beat his ass for hurting my sister." He broke off a piece of the scone and ate it. "I was stupid for how I acted before but I'll make it up to you and your men. If I had known before you arrived with them—especially under the circumstances—I don't think it would have ever gotten to this. Everything slammed at me at once; I didn't know how to handle it. So I lashed out at you, Aiden, and the others."

"I was going to tell you during that lunch that we planned. Ever since, things always came up and it never seemed the right time. I'll admit that Dad came to me and asked me to go interview them for our service, but he told me to keep it quiet. Not only from you but from everyone. It wasn't even to be in the computer system. When I realized they didn't want or need my services any longer, that I was the woman for them, I didn't know how to tell you." She smirked at him over her coffee mug. "I had expected a different reaction from you, though."

"My sister dating a man I've followed his whole career. Yeah, even I would have expected something different. Hopefully he won't hold this against me."

"Paris." She turned to find Aiden in the doorway. "I hate to interrupt, but you need to see this." He held up a stack of newspapers."

"Oh no…please tell me it's not bad."

"Bad…well, I guess that could be a way to look at it. I'm thinking disastrous might be a better way to put it." He placed the papers in front of her and the headline on the first one made her gasp. There on the front page was her being embraced by her men in the hospital hallway. Aiden and Cody on either side of her and Kain standing at her back. Whoever had taken the picture had been in the secure area, which the guards had been protecting. That could only mean a hospital staff member had taken the picture.

Aiden placed a hand on her shoulder. "The top half of every one of them reads the same: *Beyond Monogamy's daughter to strike and claim.*"

"The others?" She couldn't even look through the stack of papers. She thought when the news hit about her and her men that she'd be fine with it. After all, she was used to dealing with the media. Only this time it was different. It wasn't the publicity because of her parents' relationship, or the battle that went on for years to legalize this lifestyle, it was directed at her.

Aiden knelt beside her and took her hand into his. "It would seem as if Kings has decided to go after us in other ways. He went to the media with what happened, his false claims, even going as far as to say Kain was the one responsible for the murder of his mistress."

"What? His wife confessed."

"He tells the media that it was Kain who told his wife of the mistress and that's what sent her there. It gets crazier the more you read the article but the tabloids loved it. If people didn't pick it up for the sports attorney, former football player, or former baseball player they picked the papers up because of you and your family."

"Shit, they must be rolling in dough." London leaned forward, sifting through the papers.

"I'm sure they are, and I hate to tell you this but…the media is camped out at the gate. More are arriving every moment." Aiden rubbed his thumb across her knuckles as she gaped in disbelief. "I'm sorry, beautiful, but we're going to have a bumpy journey for a little while."

"Which is about to get worse," Kain announced from the doorway.

"How?" She wasn't sure she even wanted to know but the question was asked before she could take it back.

"I told you I was the second chair lawyer on the trial. I just received word the other lawyer was killed last night, that's why Kings was here." Kain made his way over to the table, poured himself a cup of coffee, and took a long drink. "I just received the call about it a minute ago. There's a video recording from the security camera and now they've issued a warrant for his arrest."

"Revenge will make you do crazy things." London polished off his scone before grabbing another and offering the box to Aiden and Kain who each took one.

"He gets out of prison for a murder he didn't commit and goes out to commit murder." She shook her head, unable to process it. "My God. He'll end up in the same place he just got out of. It's crazy. I would have thought he'd cherish life more, go after the people who put him there in a way that hurts their pocketbooks." She pushed the rest of her scone away, unable to think of food any longer.

"It would have made sense since the wife took everything when she divorced him. Not that he needed much considering he was looking at spending the rest of his life in prison," Kain agreed. "Until he gets caught, I think I need to keep distance between us. I won't see any of you hurt because of me."

"Out of the question." Aiden rose from where he had knelt beside her. "We're stronger together and I won't have you off by yourself. I know you, you'll try to be a one man army and bring him down yourself. Absolutely not."

"He's right." She held her other hand out to Kain, who immediately took it. "You're safer here than anywhere else. I won't have you out there by yourself. Remember, we're all together in this."

"Paris is right, this house is safer than anywhere else for you." London topped off his coffee. "If there's a murderer out there gunning for you, it's best you're here."

"That's a change of attitude." Aiden glanced toward London.

"Let's just say I've seen the light." He pushed the papers aside and looked at Kain, then to Aiden. "I think it's time we come up with a game plan. After all, we are all on the same side. We want to keep Paris happy and safe. If one of you gets hurt it's going to hurt her. So as my dads always drilled into our heads, no one goes anywhere without a guard. Got that?"

"Aiden and Paris are used to guards but not me. My work is confidential…"

"We're not talking about when you're meeting with a client, on the phone, or anything like that." She glanced up at Kain. "You need protection, all of us do. If he comes after us, I want to know you're safe. We'll have enough issues with the media. We need to make sure our backs our covered from all angles, that includes watching the windows for shooters waiting for us to come out."

He started to say something but she ran her hand over his cheek. "My cowboy, I won't have something happen to you because you're stubborn."

Over the next hour, they had worked out a plan that made everyone happy, and kept them safe. Paris leaned against the counter and rolled her shoulders, completely tensed as if she had been in some extreme contract negotiations. Before she could suggest something to relieve the stress, Schwartz walked in the back door.

"Hey, Schwartz, let me bring you up to speed on the situation," London called to him.

"I've got some calls to make." Kain rose and stood beside her. "Give me twenty minutes and we can go see your mom if you want."

"I might need longer than that; I need to speak with Schwartz. Where's Cody anyway?"

"He was checking with some of the contacts I have to see if anyone has seen or heard from Kings. I suspect he's still in your office working. Do you want me to send him down?"

"No, it's fine." She missed having him by her side but what he was doing was more important.

When Kain placed a kiss on her lips and stepped away, Aiden moved next to her. "I should also bring the two newest guards up to speed. Schwartz and the two guards we brought in will have the primary protection detail for us, especially you, today."

"I'm fine, go ahead. Then we can go see Mom." She looked over Aiden's shoulder to London and added. "All of us. Together."

"Yes, sister dearest."

She busied herself with the dishes, rinsing them before adding them to the dishwasher, while London and Schwartz talked. She tried to get her thoughts off everything that was going on and figure out what she was going to tell Schwartz. Whatever happened with his sister, she needed to discuss his job with him now that he was the guardian of his niece. She needed to know if he was willing to continue as her guard and what his plans for his niece were. She also hoped to find out why he hadn't told her what was going on.

"Hey, Paris." Schwartz leaned against the counter next to the dishwasher. "You know I've got you covered, so try not to stress too much. Focus on Mrs. Nelson and your family."

"I'd never doubted you." She closed the dishwasher and turned it on. "Come with me, there's something I wanted to discuss with you." Without waiting for him to follow, she led the way to Paul's office. Normally she'd have used hers, but with Cody and Kain using it she needed another space that would give them privacy.

"What's going on?" he asked when she shut the door behind them.

"Have a seat." She motioned to the small sitting area because this was

169

supposed to be a friendly conversation, not one with her as his boss.

"I'm not sure I like where this is going." He took a seat in the only chair, leaving the loveseat for her.

"Beating around the bush is pointless, so I'll come right to the point. Why didn't you tell me about your family?" When he only raised his eyebrow at her, as if wondering what she knew, she continued. "I found out this morning that you went to court on Friday to gain custody of your niece because your sister can't care for her. You should have told me."

"Why? So you can let me go from a job I love that gives me the ability to provide a life for her? What would happen then? I'll tell you what, she'd be stuck in the same shitty system I was raised in." There was a heat in his eyes she hadn't seen before.

"Why would I fire you because you did the right thing by your family? Do you think so little of me that I would just let you go? You're an excellent guard and you saved my life. I'd hate to lose you because I know you keep me safe and you do your best to keep bystanders out of the line of crap that seems to be following my family." She leaned forward, placing her elbows on her knees. "I thought I was more than your employer, or your assignment…damn it, Schwartz I thought we were friends."

"We are, and I never meant to hurt you. I didn't tell you because I've come to see you and your family as my family. You know I have no one. Growing up in the system my sister and I were separated, it wasn't until she was pregnant with Mya that we even found each other." He ran his hand over his jawline. "To take the chance of losing you guys was something I wasn't willing to risk. I had hoped to keep the situation with Mya quiet until I could prove it wouldn't interfere with my job."

"I don't know the whole story about your past, but I can guess it was rough. I know you had a few brushes with the law as a juvenile before you turned toward boxing and martial arts. It's the reason we found you. You've come a long way since then, whether it be because of your history or your training, or both, you're a damn fine guard."

"If you're not firing me, then why am I here?"

"I wanted to talk to you about this. I need to know if you have things in line in order to continue doing your job, or if you need some time off to get things done."

He shook his head. "Everything has been covered. I hired a nanny, Riley, more than two months ago to make sure Mya and her would work, and it's also something my lawyer suggested because it would help with the court date. She moved into my house last week to be prepared and Mya was able to come home Friday after the hearing. Everyone is settled in and Riley understands my schedule, so she'll handle everything for as long as you need me."

She ran her hands down her jeans and stood. She strolled to the window and glanced toward the gate where she could see reporters' vans and the guards arguing with someone. "This is a sensitive question, but have you considered what will happen to Mya if you're hurt or worse because of this job?"

"Somewhat."

"What do you mean?" She turned to look at him. "It's something you should have in place."

"Actually, I was hoping I could impose." He stood from the chair and came to her. "Paris, like you said we're friends…the closest friend I have, and the only one I'd want to raise Mya if something happened to me. I'd like to have Mr. Nelson draw up a will naming you Mya's guardian."

"What?" She couldn't believe what she was hearing. "You know how dangerous my life is. How could you want to place her in my care?"

"I also know you're the best one to raise her. When I took this job I didn't believe relationships could work, let alone the ones your family lives, but I've seen them firsthand. A relationship isn't something I've had much luck with, it was kind of hard, especially because I couldn't tell anyone I dated what my work was. Then, once it became legal…let's just say dating wasn't possible at all. The point is, if things change in the future, I would be open to a relationship like your parents have and like you have now. I'd like Mya to see what it's like as well so she doesn't grow up with any prejudices about it. Will you agree to be Mya's guardian if something should happen to me?"

Chapter Seventeen

Paris wasn't sure how long she stood there considering what Schwartz had asked until she finally nodded. "I'll have Dad draw up the papers. He's the one who should have been representing you in court."

"I couldn't have him as my lawyer unless I told you. We both know it's not a secret Mathew would have dealt with. He'd have wanted me to tell you in order for him to represent me. Anyway, it worked out." His lips curled up into a smile that lit up the room before he got serious. "Do you think you should tell those guys before you sign any papers? I understand if their comments on the situation will change your mind about Mya. After all, I hadn't expected you to fall for a client. You've always been so business-minded. London, on the other hand—"

"No, I'll tell them, but things won't change. They'll understand. Now, I want to see this little girl as soon as things calm down. Well, I'm not sure my life has ever been calm, but maybe Kings will be arrested quickly and we won't have that hanging over our heads any longer."

"I have a friend on the force. I'll give him a call and see if they have any leads."

"Thanks." She glanced back outside before stepping away from the window. "I'm going to see Aiden, Kain, and Cody. They might have made progress with their connections and I want to let them know what happened here. When you're done, you can meet up with the other two guards in the living room to go over your strategy for today and the trip to the hospital. They already know you're in charge."

"Who requested that?" He pulled his cell phone from his pocket but didn't unlock the screen.

"Me. I don't know these two new guys. They arrived last night and have done security detail for Aiden. However, you I know and I won't have anyone else in charge, not with all this shit hovering around, ready to drop at a moment's notice."

"I have no doubt you'll keep them on their toes." He shook his head.

"I hope they know what they're getting into," she teased, strolling from the room in search of her men. Updates were needed and then they could be on their way to the hospital. She came around the corner toward the stairs and ran straight into Kain.

"Darling, I was just coming to find you."

"You found me." She ran her hand along the tight contours of his chest. The shirt was between them but didn't stand in the way from her remembering just what was under the thin material. "Everything okay?"

"Paul called and somehow your mother managed to convince Doctor Tobias and Doctor Vander that the best place for her is here. She'll be discharged this afternoon so he just wants us to wait here for them."

"I see. Dad thinks I'm going to remain a prisoner at home now that things have come out. I'm sure that's one of the reasons Mom pressed to come home." She stepped back, anger sparked within her.

"Maybe partially, but you can't blame them for that. We all want to keep you safe." He ran his hand along her cheek. "I think it also has to do with the intruder in Mrs. Nelson's room last night."

"What?"

"Paul had stepped out of the room to get more coffee, while Mathew and your mother slept. When he came back someone had gotten past the hospital guards and was entering her room."

She took a deep breath and reminded herself that her mother was okay. "What about our guards? Mom should have had one at the room. The damn hospital security guards don't understand the dangers from people against us. They've tried over and over again to use us as examples of what will happen to those who choose to live this lifestyle."

"The guard your family hired was grabbing a bite to eat, he was only to be gone a few minutes. They had two hospital guards in as replacement for one of your guys, plus there were others farther down the hall to hold off the reporters."

"What happened? Was she harmed?"

"No, Paul arrived back just as it happened. It's the reason the hospital and doctors agreed to her discharge. They don't want to have to worry about her safety, or any of the other families, while your mother is on hospital premises." He lightly wrapped his arms around her waist. "Why are you looking so worried? It's good that she's coming home."

She nodded. "But something could have happened—"

"Don't." He let go of her and put a finger to her lips. "You can't think of what *might* have happened. The important thing is it *didn't* happen. Everyone learned from it and in the future extra precaution will be taken. What matters is she's safe."

"She could have been killed." She continued to force air into her lungs to try to ease the tightness in her chest. "Damn it why can't people see that we have the right to live however we want. We shouldn't be hated or attacked because we don't choose the standard one male and one female relationship. The world has come to accept same sex couples, so why can't they accept us?"

"Darling, same sex marriages became legal over a hundred years ago but it

175

took decades for people to accept it. We're still on the battlegrounds for this. Hopefully, one day our children will be able to live without a threat hanging over their heads. But right now we must stand strong to give future generations an opportunity to have what we've held dear."

She knew he was right, but at that moment she wanted to take her men back to Cody's plane and fly them away somewhere safe. To hide away in the middle of nowhere, where they didn't have to worry about threats to their lives, or the media, and they could just focus on each other. That could never be her life. No matter where she went, they'd always find her. Her family was leading the world beyond monogamy, and it wasn't something she could hide from even if she wanted to.

The day had gone unlike anything Paris expected. When Mom arrived back from the hospital, she seemed like a whole new person. For the first time in months she wasn't sick, she had a little more energy, and she finally had color in her cheeks. Paris wasn't sure why the cancer was just gone. Could it have been the chemotherapy and radiation combination? Or was this an honest miracle?

Even the doctors couldn't understand what had happened. Either way, none of the family was willing to look a gift horse in the mouth. They'd take this blessing and be thankful. If there was one thing cancer taught them, it was to cherish every moment as if it was their last.

They had spent much of the day together as a family, chatting in the living room, with a raging fire going. It was a perfect day together with the snow falling steadily outside. Aiden, Kain, and Cody had fit perfectly into her family as if they were always supposed to be there. Even London had joined them, his attitude diminished. They couldn't have had a better day together, without any of the pressures, if they had planned it that way.

She had even used that time with her family all together to bring them up to speed on Schwartz's situation and to ask Mathew to draw up the needed paperwork for her to have guardianship of Mya if something should happen to Schwartz. Everyone had the same reaction as she did, that he should have told them from the beginning. In the end, it had worked out, just as everything else had lately.

Now that her fathers had forced Mom to their room in order to rest, Paris sat curled up with her laptop. Aiden was on one side of her, his arm around her shoulders, while Kain worked on his laptop on the other side of her. Her sweet exhausted Cody had fallen asleep on the chair across from her.

"I thought you had work to do? Instead I find you eyeing Cody," Aiden whispered, so not to wake him.

"Oh, you mean these dozens of client emails? Hmmm, here I thought they'd answer themselves." She slipped her finger over the mouse pad and brought up the next email. It was a message from Carter about the match she had set up for him. It explained how wonderful things were going and that they couldn't have been happier. He'd also mentioned an invitation to their wedding in June, while the official invitation would be sent out later. Things had worked out for them—another successful match.

"Paris." Mathew stood in the doorway.

"Dad, come in. Everything okay?" She leaned forward, placing her laptop on the ottoman.

"Mom's fine, she's having ice cream in bed with Paul. I need to discuss the company with you."

"Okay, we can go into my office." She started to get up before he stopped her.

"This is something that will affect them as well so we might as well do it here." He sat in the only other chair, his elbows on his knees. "Paul and I haven't been involved nearly as much as we should be with the company."

"That's understandable, Dad, you needed to focus on Mom."

"I could have sworn I wasn't finished." He shook his head, but smiled at her. "Paris, you've shown that you have what it takes to run the company. You have ideas to keep it fresh and attractive to all generations. While we still want to have a part in the company, we also want to do more with Amy. Therefore, we want you to step into the position of vice-president of Beyond Monogamy."

Completely stunned, her jaw slacked open and she had to blink away the tears of joy to focus. "I don't know what to say."

"Say yes. You've worked long and hard for this company. It's time you begin to take it over. Our goal all along was for you to take the company someday, and for London to be vice-president. These are the first steps to it." Dad leaned back in his chair. "With you taking over the day to day operations, and other vice-presidential duties, that means London will need to step into the roles of some of the things you used to handle. It will give him the chance to prove himself and grow up. I'm not giving you this VP promotion because you're my daughter, but because you deserve this opportunity."

He glanced at Aiden and Kain before looking back at her. "It doesn't mean you have to stay here. If they're your destiny and you wish to move to Wyoming, you can do everything you need to there. However, there is one stipulation to this promotion."

She rose an eyebrow at him. "What's that?"

"You have to hire an assistant. No deal without one. You were overworked before and I won't see you that way again as VP." He ran his hands down the armrest and stood. "You don't have to give me an answer now."

"I'll take it, and I know the perfect person for the assistant position."

Dad stood in front of the chair and shoved his hands in the pocket. "Who?" When she told him, he gaped. "Schwartz?" The surprise was clear in his tone.

"He'd be perfect at it. In the past he's done a few things for me and it makes sense with this new development," she explained.

"He's your best guard." Aiden's teased his fingers along her shoulder.

"True, which makes it an even better idea to have him by my side as my assistant. It also allows him to have more reasonable hours to care for Mya. It's best for both of us."

"You expect him to do double duty? To be your assistant and your bodyguard?" Mathew asked.

"Yes, somewhat. If something happens, wouldn't it be better to have him by my side? It would also make the clients feel more at ease if they think he's just my assistant instead of a bodyguard." She tipped her head to look at Aiden. "There's also the other two guards you brought in, so it's not like I'll be unprotected. We can see how they work out and Schwartz can train them to take over as my lead guards."

"Talk to him and find out if he's interested, but you damn well better be safe." Mathew looked to the guys. "I trust the three of you can make sure she thinks this through completely before she talks to Schwartz."

"Leave it to us." Aiden nodded.

"Why is it that men always stick together?" She shook her head. "Dad, you know I can take care of myself."

"I also know that without Schwartz you'd have been in worse situations in the past. He's kept some of the shit at bay to keep you safe." Mathew paused for a moment before finally nodding. "I can see some benefits to having him as your assistant."

"I agree there are some benefits to it." Kain didn't even look up from his laptop.

"I'm glad someone is on my side. Schwartz—" Her words were cut off by a loud explosion, the house shaking. "What the hell was that?"

Cody practically flew out of the chair where he'd been sleeping. "What the fuck was that?"

"Paris, where's your pistol?" Mathew snapped, stepping toward the window but keeping his body low.

"Locked in my nightstand." She stood and went to him, only to be pushed back.

"Shit. Stay the hell away from the windows." He reached over and turned off the light. "Get your gun, and keep low. If the guys don't have their own and know how to use them, give them one."

"Everyone okay up there?" Paul called out.

"They're fine. Don't you dare go out that door, Paul!" Mathew looked to Paris who was grabbing the weapons she had and handing them to the men. "Don't leave this damn room for any reason."

Kain peaked out through the curtain and mumbled something, but all she caught was, "Because of me…"

"Kain?"

"It's Kings. He blew up your main entrance." He stepped away from the window and looked at the pistol she had handed him.

"Don't think of it." Mathew stepped into his way. "There are security guards dealing with the situation. I won't have you risking yourself."

"He's here because of me. I won't have Paris or any of you harmed because of me. Don't stand there and tell me you wouldn't do the same." Kain and Mathew glared at each other.

"Kain, please…" she begged, not wanting him to get hurt because of this.

"Cody, stay with Paris," Aiden ordered before shoving a loaded magazine into the handgun she'd given him. "We'll be fine."

"This is insane." She tried to reason, to hold back the fear that was blooming inside of her. The gunfire, and screams from outside, neared the house.

"Paris, whatever happens, stay here." Mathew left the room with Aiden and Kain on his heels.

"Don't!" She cried out one last time but they were gone.

"Shh, love." Cody wrapped his arms around her. "It's going to be okay. They'll be fine."

"You don't know that." Her legs gave out from under her. If it wasn't for Cody easing them down onto the floor, she'd have collapsed.

Two manly figures stepped into the doorway causing Paris and Cody to point their guns in that direction. "Aiden sent us." Oliver stepped into the room, his hands in front of him.

"Shit. You could have gotten yourself killed." Paris lowered her gun. "What the hell is going on downstairs? Is my family safe?"

"Paul and London are with your mother. Mathew said he was going to check on them."

"What about Aiden and Kain?" she snapped when Oliver left them out.

"They were going out the front door as I came up."

"No!" She tried to wiggle from Cody's embrace to get to the window, in case she could see anything.

"Love, just stay here. I don't want you any closer to the windows, it's too dangerous." He kept the gun in his hand but wrapped both arms around her. "Has anyone called the police?"

"A guard came in from outside and called when things started to go down. We were protecting the main entrance when Aiden assigned us up here," Oliver explained. "Miss Nelson, I'd prefer if you'd come farther away from the windows. From where you're sitting you could be a target for a stray bullet, and you're in perfect eyesight of the doorway if anyone should make it this far."

She let Cody move her across the room near the bathroom door, so they were more protected. The farther she got from the door, the harder it was to understand what people were yelling downstairs. She thought she could hear Kain's voice but she couldn't be sure.

"Paris..." Cody used his finger to turn her head toward him and she realized he had been calling her name for some time. "Look at me."

"What?" She tried to focus but everything seemed to be happening in a haze.

"Love, I've got to go help them. You're safe here."

"No, please." She grabbed a handful of his shirt. "Don't go."

"I have to. I can't sit here and do nothing when they're in danger. I've spent too many years as Aiden's guard to stop now." He pried her fingers from his shirt and kissed the top of her hand. "I promise all of us will be back safe."

Tears poured from her eyes without an end in sight. The three men she loved with everything in her were in danger and she was unable to do anything. She clutched the gun she'd placed on the floor beside her, and pushed herself off the floor to stand. "I won't sit here doing nothing."

Chapter Eighteen

Paris took a deep breath, trying to loosen her muscles. If she needed to use her weapon, she had to be relaxed. If every muscle was tight from stress she'd be off target. Being off target was the last thing she needed.

"Miss Nelson, don't do this." Oliver came closer, shoving his gun into his holster.

"I'm not doing anything but going to the aid of my family. I won't sit up here. My whole family, the men I love, they're all downstairs."

"I'll keep you here by force if I have to. I have direct orders not to let you out of my sight."

"You'll have to knock me unconscious or kill me to stop me." As soon as she moved, his arm shot out, wrapping around her waist. He lifted her completely off the floor with barely any strain.

"I told you, you're not leaving." Even as she fought, he held her tight, her feet off the ground.

"Damn it put me the hell down."

"Do I have your word you won't do anything stupid?"

"Since when is saving your family stupid?" she snapped.

"There are ten or twelve guards on the property since the reporters began to show up, yet they're not enough to protect your family, and somehow you're going to stop them. Is that what I'm supposed to understand?"

"Would you do the same if it was your family?"

"No." He lowered her to the ground but didn't loosen his grip around her waist. "I'd put together a plan of action before rushing off hot-headed. Otherwise, someone will get hurt."

"Plan." She nodded, his words finally making her think clearly. Sirens echoed in the distance, coming to the rescue.

Gunshots reverberated through the house as Oliver let go of her and stepped in front of her. The other guard, whose name she couldn't remember at the moment, turned toward the door as if expecting someone. With the echoes of gunshots, the fear raced inside her, making her stomach turn. Screams echoed and her heart broke knowing something had gone wrong.

Without thinking, she pushed Oliver back. She must have startled him because he wasn't able to catch her before she could make it out of the room. She checked the hall, easing down the steps with her gun pointed in front of her, ready to shoot before she could be shot. Nothing. The living room was empty, giving her a chance to make it down the steps without any problems.

"Paris, get back here." Oliver had caught up, fear and anger evident in his whispers.

She ignored him, descended the last step, and peeked around the corner. The front door was wide open, giving her a clear view outside, and the security lights cast a yellow glow. That was when she saw it. Kain's blood coated his white dress shirt while Aiden applied pressure to his shoulder.

"What the hell happened?" Without looking to make sure it was clear, she rushed out of the house to his side, tears rolling down her cheeks.

"Where's…" Aiden looked behind her and his eyes burned with anger. "This is what you call protection? Oliver, you were supposed to protect her."

"Instead of ripping me a new one, how about a status update. There's plenty of time to chew me out later." Oliver glanced around the room, his gun held at the ready. "Is she in danger now?"

"Kings is dead." Cody took the gun from Paris's trembling hand. "You two can join the guards and police outside keeping the reporters at bay. We'll discuss this later."

"You're hurt." She laid her hand over Aiden's and pulled the towel back. "How bad is it?"

"The damn bastard is lucky, it's just his shoulder. Kings was a lousy shot," Aiden answered.

"You didn't know what you were walking into. Damn it, Paris you should have stayed upstairs," Kain bitched.

"I'm glad to see you too." She pressed a little harder on his shoulder, making him grunt in pain. "I knew something happened and I could hear the screaming. I knew someone was hurt."

Cody rubbed her shoulder. "We're fine, love."

"Fine! This is not fine." She pulled the towel away, instantly regretting it as she could see the hole in his shirt, blood pouring from it. Her hand shook until she almost dropped the towel. Aiden placed his hand over it and pressed it against Kain's shoulder again.

"I'm fine, Paris, really. It's just a scratch." Kain tried to convince her, but he was failing miserably. He slumped on the porch bench, appearing pale, as the blood seeped from his chest.

"We're all alive, that's what matters." Aiden placed his free hand on her back. "Come on, beautiful, deep breaths. It's over now."

"Until next time." She glanced from each of the men before looking down at the blood soaked ground. "What am I supposed to do if something happens to one of you?"

"Darling, we can't think like that," Kain said, his eyes closed.

"Remember, cherish every day." Cody repeated her words from earlier.

"At least the threat of Kings is over," Aiden reminded her.

"There will be something else to take its place." If it wasn't Kings, it would be the next lunatic out for blood because of her family's reputation.

"What the fuck happened here?" Schwartz strolled toward them, leaving the cops outside and a few lingering in the kitchen. "I leave to go home to check on Mya and you not only have an explosion, but there's blood everywhere. Paris, are you hurt?"

"It's not my blood…Kain's." The last bit of her energy gone, she sank down onto the bench next to him.

"We're going to have to answer questions. Don't let her out of your sight." Aiden glared at him. "Do you hear that Paris? You stay with him and listen to him. I don't want to see you running through whatever trouble finds us next because you think something has happened to us. It's not okay to get yourself hurt or worse yet, killed. We'll take care of this, watch each other's backs, and when it's over we'll come back to you. I promise."

"That's not a promise you can keep," she whispered but the argument was cut off before it got started when a police officer approached them.

"The paramedics will be right over." The young officer looked over each of the men. "We're going to need everyone's statements while we try to determine what happened here and who fired the fatal shot."

"That was me," Cody stated, gaining the officer's attention. "After he shot Kain I had no choice but to return fire."

"Very well, the detective will want to speak with you first. We'll get to all of you." He turned to Kain. "I'll have an officer meet you at the hospital for your statement."

"He's not going anywhere." Mathew stepped out of the house. "I have our family doctor on his way to attend to him. No one will be giving statements without legal representation, either. My partner Mr. Harmon has just arrived and he'll sit in with everyone."

"Mr. Nelson, that's not necessary," Aiden said.

"Actually, I think it is." Mathew glanced at Paris. "You're family now."

"I was upstairs, I didn't see anything."

"The detective might still wish to question you," the officer told her.

"I'm not leaving him." She glanced down at all the blood covering the towel and her hands. "Dad, where's the doctor? He can't wait…"

"I'm okay, darling." Kain tipped his head to lay it on top of hers.

"Sir, if you'll come with me, we can get started." The officer nodded toward the detective.

"Mr. Harmon," Mathew called and pointed at Cody.

With a quick kiss, Cody was gone and she sat there wondering what would have happened if he hadn't come to their aid. Would Kain or Aiden have been killed? Her sweet Cody, the one who seemed the most innocent of her men, had killed someone. He'd done it to protect her, the men she loved, her family, and the guards. Still, he had risked himself when he could have stayed upstairs with her and that was what scared her. What happened if they weren't so lucky next time? How could she live without her men? Even if she only lost one of them, it would break her heart.

The fireplace crackled, sending sparks up the chimney. Even with the roaring fire, Paris couldn't chase the chill away. It wasn't from cold weather, but the fear she had experienced for the first time tonight. It had been hours since the attack but her thoughts wouldn't be steered from it, at least not for long. The danger she had grown up with was different now that she was in love, because it meant it could cost her even more than before.

With a blanket around her shoulders, she sat on the edge of the sofa where Kain dozed. The pain pill did its best to knock him out, yet he fought it to comfort her. She knew he would be fine, Doctor Vander had assured her the wound would heal without any lasting damage, but still she couldn't shake the thought she could have lost any one of them that night.

"Paris." Aiden stood by her side, his hand on her shoulder. "Why don't we get some sleep? Kain should be resting in bed."

"Yeah…yeah. Help him to bed; I'll be up in a bit."

"No." Kain wrapped his hand around her wrist as she started to move away. "I'm staying with you. You need all of us right now."

"You're not in very good condition," Cody reminded him. "Let me help you to the bed. You can rest and we'll comfort her. Tomorrow when the drugs have worked their way through your system, you can show her you're fine."

"He's right, you need your rest." Tears prickled behind her eyelids and she tried to blink them away.

"No, darling, I need to be with you." Kain reached up with his good arm, drawing his fingers over her cheek. "I love you."

"I love you, too." She brushed the tears away with the back of her hand. "I'm sorry, I don't know what's wrong with me."

"You thought you lost us tonight, you're allowed to be emotional." Cody leaned forward from the chair he had taken beside the sofa. "You're not getting rid of us, love."

"I thought I understood what it was like to deal with this shit, but until I found you I didn't realize it. It's not like I don't love Mom, my dads, or London, because I do. It's just different with you." She couldn't explain it but for the first time she truly understood what terror was like.

Kain glanced up to Aiden. "I think it's time."

Cody nodded in Aiden's direction as well, forcing her to turn to him. "What's going on?"

"Beautiful, I had wanted this to be romantic but maybe they're right." Aiden came around her until he could kneel in front of her. "Since you walked into our lives a few months ago, we knew you were the woman we wanted to spend the rest of our lives with. We thought we'd have a bigger fight on our

188

hands to convince you, but you were open to it from the beginning. You've made us fall head over heels in love with you, and none of us would change that. Paris Nelson, will you do us the honor of being our wife?" He opened a small black box, tugging out a beautiful princess cut diamond ring in white gold.

Tears freely flowed down her face, only this time they were happy ones. "Yes." She used her right hand to cup his cheek as he slid the engagement ring on her left ring finger. "I would be honored to be your wife...all of you."

Kain slid his uninjured arm around her waist. "We've waited all our lives for you and now we finally have you. Don't think for one minute we'll let you get away with another stunt like you pulled tonight."

"I know you didn't want me to leave you," Cody began, "but Oliver wouldn't have let anything happen to you. I couldn't be sure about the safety of everyone else." He nodded to Kain, who sank back against the cushions again. "See, he ended up getting shot because he didn't have me."

"Screw...you." Kain's words were slurred from the drugs.

"He shot before Cody got to us. I had my pistol aimed but he had ducked behind a car, leaving me waiting for a shot," Aiden explained, nodding to Cody. "He came out just as Kings stood to take another shot."

"I killed him in our defense. He'd have killed us if I hadn't gotten him first." The way Cody said the words it make her wonder if he was doing it to convince himself or them.

She rose from where she was sitting and went to Cody, curling into his lap, and wrapped her arms around his neck. "My love, you saved all of us tonight by taking that shot. There is nothing to be upset about. You're my hero."

"I killed a man..." He shook his head, as if he still couldn't believe it.

"You saved my life," Kain mumbled. The pills had him almost completely knocked out.

"Come on, let's go to bed. I think we could all use a little cuddling and sleep." She stood and tugged his hand.

"I'm injured; doesn't that mean I get to lay next to my beautiful fiancée?" Kain didn't even open his eyes or move. "Actually maybe...I'll sleep...here."

"No, buddy, you need a bed. Tonight you and Cody can sleep next to her, after all I think you both need her the most." Aiden winked at her and leaned down to help Kain sit up. "This relationship is all about compromise and we're all in this together. Tonight is about touches, cuddles, and forgetting the awful shit that has happened. Tonight is about us. Tomorrow we'll deal with the rest of the world."

"I couldn't have said it better myself." She needed to hold her men, to know they were safe, as much as they needed to hold her. These men were her life, and if she had lost even one of them tonight her heart would have broken. She didn't have favorites or love one more than another, she loved and needed all of them. Soon, they'd be her husbands.

 # Epilogue

Cool air drifted around Paris, blowing her hair into her face. She didn't bother to push it away, instead she stood there watching her husbands with their families. This was the first barbeque of the summer, and they were holding the event in their new house. It was extra special since Aiden and Kain's family had joined them as well. Everyone was joking and chatting as if they'd known each other for years. There was something special about a family living beyond the terms of monogamy. Paris felt they cherished times together that other families didn't have.

Dividing their time between Wyoming and Colorado had required them to buy a second home. Even though this one wasn't custom built as the one in Wyoming had been, it still became their home, and more importantly, it was less than a mile from her family's house. It was still a ranch style house, with lots of land, but somewhat smaller. They didn't each have the dedicated office spaces they had at the other place. This one only had four bedrooms, not that it mattered since most nights they all slept together, rotating so no one person was always stuck on the outside.

Everything had come together almost perfectly. She had found three amazing men she was destined to spend the rest of her life with. Mom's cancer was gone and hopefully for good this time. London was still adjusting to his new role within the company, but now that she was only around part time there was only Dottie for him to fall back on and she wasn't cutting him any slack.

Schwartz had accepted the position as her assistant with some reservations. He had been against it at first and accused her of using it as a way to get him out of the line of danger so he'd make it home to Mya. They had some heated discussions about it, but in the end it had been Cody who had convinced him he was perfect for it. With this new position, Schwartz, Mya, and the nanny were stuck traveling back and forth as well. This time when they returned to Wyoming there would be a new house just off the mountain on their land for Schwartz and his family. This had been Aiden's idea to keep him close in case anything should happen since they all firmly stood against having round-the-clock guards.

Their security wasn't as big of a deal in Thermopolis, Wyoming, as it was here because the community was smaller, and where they lived no one had a reason to be there unless they were coming to the house. Aiden, Kain, and Cody had bought up all the surrounding land around the house, giving them all the privacy they could ask for.

Schwartz stepped through the sliding glass door with Mya in hand and Riley just a few steps behind him. "Mya's been putting up a fuss today, wanting to see you." He brushed the blonde hair from the little girl's face.

"Come see your Aunt Paris." Paris held out her arms and Mya came right to her. Schwartz had asked all the Nelsons to step in and be a family to the little girl. After all, he considered them family as well, and with Mya being raised around them, it seemed like the right thing to do. Paris loved being an Aunt. It was giving her hands-on training for her own children.

At almost two years old, Mya was still a love bug; they believed she was trying to make up for the time her mother had neglected her. Even now, Mya's mother—Schwartz's sister—had turned to drugs, leaving him alone to raise her.

"Have you figured out what you're going to do about her calling you

Daddy?"

"Oh, Paris." He shoved his hands into the pockets of his jeans. "It feels wrong."

"But that's what you are to her."

"Yeah, you're the only parent she has," Riley pointed out.

He looked between the two women. "What if my sister gets her life back together?"

"You know the chances of that." Paris hated to crush his hopes, but it was unlikely and Schwartz needed to consider that. "Even if she does, by the time she'd prove it to the courts, Mya will be old enough to understand."

"I know you're right, but it still feels wrong." He glanced back at Riley. "I'm *not* the only parent she has."

"What? You can't seriously mean—"

"No, I mean *you*. You do just as much, if not more for her." She started to say something before he cut her off again. "Don't give me that *it's just your job* stuff. I see how you are with her. If it wasn't for you, she wouldn't have adjusted as well as she has." He took her hand into his. "Thank you."

Paris watched them and wondered if something was happening between them. Riley was a sweet girl, and she'd taken to their way of life without any issues. She had been open and accepting, but she seemed so innocent compared to Schwartz.

"Darling, I need you in the house for a minute," Kain called from the doorway.

"Excuse me." She started to hand Mya back to Schwartz only to have her kick up a fit.

"Just bring her if Schwartz doesn't mind," Kain hollered over the little girl's cries.

"Go ahead, we'll grab a beer and we'll be out here." Schwartz tipped his head toward the chest of drinks by the table.

Adjusting the little girl on her hip, Paris turned to Kain. "What's going on?"

"There's someone I need you to officially meet."

She stepped into the kitchen to find a man who looked very much like Kain standing near the island in the kitchen. The only thing missing was the cowboy hat Kain favored, but the other man had the same business-like stare.

"This is my brother Jenkin, and he needs your help." Kain pulled out one of the bar stools for her and she took a seat with Mya on her lap.

"Help with what?"

"I want what Kain has." He rested his hands on the counter on either side of his hips. "Except it's not that easy."

"Love never is." She smirked and looked up at Kain. "But it's always worth it." She shared a moment with Kain before she looked back at Jenkin. "So, what is it you need my help with?"

"I was hoping you'd say that." Another man stepped into the kitchen.

Her body stilled as her gaze traveled over him. His shaggy dark brown hair fell to the bottom of his ears. His deep green eyes seem to hold a mystery she wasn't sure she wanted to unravel. She didn't recognize him, and he wasn't one of the guards.

"I'm Scott, Jenkin's husband."

She turned to Kain. "You didn't say—"

"That my brother was married to a man," Kain interrupted. "No, I didn't, but I didn't think it mattered. They've been out of the country for the last six months and I was waiting until you met him."

"It didn't…I mean, it doesn't matter." She shook her head and turned back to Jenkin and Scott. "I think we may have gotten off on the wrong foot and I'm sorry about that. It's just surprised me, that's all."

"You're not the first to be shocked." Jenkin took Scott's hand in his own. "Until I met Scott, I never knew…I'd only been with women until him."

"That's why we need your help, your company's help. Jenkin and I want to find a wife who will accept our relationship, while still allowing us to have one with her." Scott glanced at Jenkin, appearing nervous.

"Okay." Paris bounced her leg to keep Mya quiet as she thought things through.

"They're leaving in the morning with my parents, but when we get back to Wyoming at the beginning of the week, maybe you can meet with them," Kain suggested.

"You're leaving so soon?"

"We have to get back. Scott's a songwriter and has a deadline at the end of the week." Jenkin looked over at his husband, who nodded. "But next week, once you're home, we'd like to speak with you about this. That is…if you think you can help us. Kain seems to think you can."

"I can help. I have no doubt about that. I'll just need to pry into your lives. I'm not sure you want your new sister-in-law doing that."

"We have nothing to hide." Jenkin pushed off the counter. "Then we won't take up any more of your time with this today. Once you get back home and settled we look forward to hearing from you."

"Welcome to the family," Scott said. "I'm sorry I was unable to attend the wedding, I was in Scotland working with one of the artists who's using my songs on his album."

"I understand." She said goodbye to Scott and Jenkin, watching as they left. Once they were alone, she turned to Kain. "You could have told me instead of springing it on me like that."

"Actually, I didn't know until two weeks ago and I figured it was best for you to meet them in person. They eloped when Jenkin went to Scotland. Said they didn't want to wait another day." He wrapped his arm around her shoulder. "It wasn't until they arrived an hour ago that he said he wanted your help. I knew you couldn't start right now, but I wanted you to meet them and know what they wanted."

"I feel like I made a fool of myself." She slipped off the bar stool and adjusted Mya in her arms. "What a wonderful impression I made on my new brother-in-laws."

"It's not them you're married to, so who cares. Anyway, you did fine." He leaned down to kiss her just as his father popped around the corner.

"Hey, Kain, your mother is looking for you."

"Go ahead," she told him. "I'm going to get a drink and I'll be out." In reply, she received a quick kiss before he turned to go outside.

She bounced her niece up on her hip. "I made a fool of myself, but still my man loves me. When you're older make sure you find a man just like my husbands." In response, Mya cooed.

She grabbed a bottle of water from the refrigerator and headed back out to join the party. "You know, little one, you're getting heavy. Let's find your playpen and set you down."

"Here, I'll take her." Riley appeared as she glanced around to check where the playpen was set up.

"Thanks." Paris waited as Riley lifted the little girl. Turning, she began looking around for one of her men.

"Daughter, you have a glow about you. Is there anything you wish to tell me?" Mom strolled up next to her, carrying a large bowl of fruit salad. Her mother's brown hair was still short, but it was starting to fill out again now that she wasn't going through the cancer treatments, and her figure was beginning to regain the weight she had lost. No one would have suspected that just a few months ago she had been fighting for her life.

Paris instantly touched her stomach as the doctor's words played out in her mind again. *Pregnant.* She still couldn't believe it. In seven and a half months they were going to be parents. That was one of the reasons for this barbeque, so they could finally spill the news about her pregnancy with everyone gathered in one place.

"Well, Paris?" Mom pushed again when she didn't answer.

"We were going to announce it after everyone ate."

Her mother wrapped an arm around her and squealed with joy. "I'm going to be a grandmother!"

"What's going on?" Paul stopped on his way out the door. Mom turned to him, tears in her eyes.

"I thought we were going to wait." Aiden slipped his arm around her waist and tugged her closer to his body.

"Mom knew, I didn't say anything." She let her head fall back against Aiden's chest and looked up at him. Her sexy husband gleamed down at her, a twinkle in his eyes, and she knew he was just as excited to tell everyone as she was. "Well, the cat's out of the bag, let's tell them."

Aiden hollered for everyone to gather around. Kain and Cody moved beside her, knowing what was about to happen. Not only was she excited she was going to be a mother; she knew her amazing husbands would be wonderful fathers. She was also thrilled her child would be brought in a family surrounded by such love.

Her child would be able to have the extended family she hadn't had growing up. Paris wondered if she'd missed out on something special, but she knew her baby wouldn't. Her grandparents and the rest of her parents' families had disowned them when they had come out about being together. She'd be able to offer her child something she didn't have—many grandparents and other family members. London, and Kain's brother, would make great uncles as well.

She hadn't begun to show, but still she ran her hand over her stomach, knowing life was developing within her.

"My sweet child, you'll be blessed with people who care about you. Not just your parents…but everyone." She leaned into Aiden's embrace and took hold of Kain's hand. As if knowing what she wanted, Cody came to stand behind her and placed his hand on her shoulder. Her men.

"Time to party," Cody whispered, his mouth next to her ear. "Then, after everyone leaves, we'll have a party of our own. After all…there are still a few rooms we haven't *christened* yet."

Marissa Dobson

Born and and raised in the Pittsburgh, Pennsylvania area, Marissa Dobson now resides about an hour from Washington, D.C. She's a lady who likes to keep busy, and is always busy doing something. With two different college degrees, she believes you are never done learning.

Being the first daughter to an avid reader, this gave her the advantage of learning to read at a young age. Since learning to read she has always had her nose in a book. It wasn't until she was a teenager that she started writing down the stories she came up with.

Marissa is blessed with a wonderful supportive husband, Thomas. He's her other half and allows her to stay home and pursue her writing. He puts up with all her quirks and listens to her brainstorm in the middle of the night.

Her writing buddy Pup Cameron, a cocker spaniel, is always around to listen to her bounce ideas off him. He might not be able to answer, but he's helpful in his own ways.

She loves to hear from readers so send her an email at marissa@marissadobson.com or visit her online at http://www.marissadobson.com.

Other Books by Marissa Dobson

Alaskan Tigers:

Tiger Time

The Tiger's Heart

Tigress for Two

Night with a Tiger

Trusting a Tiger

Alaskan Tigers Box Set Vol. 1

Jinx's Mate

Two for Protection

Bearing Secrets

Tiger Tracks

Healing the Clan

Alaskan Tigers Box Set Vol. 2

Her Black Tiger

Tiger Trouble

Forever Creek Shifters:

Forever's Fight

Protective Forever

Stormkin:

Storm Queen

Crimson Hollow:

Romancing the Fox

Loving the Bears

A Lion's Chance

Swift Move

Purrable Lion

Bearly Alive

Saved by a Lion

Furever Mated Box Set

Reaper:

A Touch of Death

Beyond Monogamy:

Theirs to Treasure

SEALed for You:

Ace in the Hole

Explosive Passion

Operation Family

Marine for You:

Lucky Chance

Back from Hell

A Marine's Second Chance

Cedar Grove Medical:

Hope's Toy Chest

Destiny's Wish

Leena's Dream

Fate:

Snowy Fate

Sarah's Fate

Mason's Fate

As Fate Would Have It

Half Moon Harbor Resort:

Learning to Live

Learning What Love Is

Her Cowboy's Heart

Half Moon Harbor Resort Vol. 1

Tanner Cycles:

Until Sydney

Phantom Security:

Different Sides

Undercover Agent

Clearwater:

Winterbloom

Unexpected Forever

Losing to Win

Christmas Countdown

The Surrogate

Clearwater Romance Volume One

Small Town Doctor

Stand Alone:

Through Smoke

SEALed Rescue

SEALed in Texas

Starting Over

Secret Valentine

Restoring Love

www.ingramcontent.com/pod-product-compliance
Lightning Source LLC
Chambersburg PA
CBHW050934120626
46552CB00001B/205

* 9 7 8 1 9 3 9 9 7 8 5 6 1 *